The English Prince and the Enemies to Lovers – a R

Annie Gordon

Chapter One

He woke up to the smell of bacon. The aroma momentarily confused him. He didn't eat bacon. He didn't buy it, and he knew that he didn't have any in his fridge. That was when he remembered he wasn't in his own apartment.

Where was he? Before he forced his eyes open, he said a silent prayer – *please let me be alone in bed... please, pretty please...*

He reached out a tentative hand, and relief flooded through him when he realised that he was fully clothed, under a quilt in a single-sized bed. *Thank you, God.*

So – despite his rather drunken night out - he hadn't staggered home with some woman he'd picked up at the club. He wondered if that meant something. Perhaps, being a nearly married man, was rubbing off on him? His mother *would* be pleased.

Fierce sunshine battered its way through the flimsy curtains and mercilessly stabbed his eyeballs. He screwed his eyes against the glare and surveyed the room. Judging by the Spiderman wallpaper, scattered toys, and the huge teddy bear in bed with him – he was in the bedroom of his best friend's son. Once again, his friend had rescued him. Jacob deserved a medal... or a knighthood. *He* could knight him. *Why not? He didn't need anybody's permission.*

Thankfully, Jacob's wife and son were in Scotland, or his friend wouldn't have dared to bring him home. The last time he'd crashed there, Patricia, Jacob's wife, hadn't been terribly impressed. Patricia was formidable. She stood barely five foot tall in her stockinged feet, was so slim that a breeze would blow her away, but she had a voice that could fell you at fifty paces. She had threatened divorce if her hapless husband inflicted him on her again. Louis believed her and, more importantly,

Jacob believed her. Friendship, or not, if Patricia had been home, Louis would've had to fend for himself.

He wasn't good at fending for himself. He'd never had to, and he would have got home safely without Jacob's help. That's what his royal protection detail was for.

Forget the knighthood. His friend hadn't really done anything to deserve it. In fact – if his memory served him correctly – he recalled Jacob preventing him from attending a very inviting rendezvous with a delectable, rather famous, model.

Ah, but the paparazzi. How could he forget how close he'd come to being plastered all over the front pages yet again? If they'd succeeded in feasting their cameras on him, not only would his mother be most displeased, but he'd scupper any chance he had of persuading Felicity to marry him.

Jacob had extracted him with military precision - got him right out of there right under the noses of the press.

Good old Jacob. He definitely deserved that knighthood.

It was a relief to have Jacob as a friend. He was so normal. He lived in a terraced house in a leafy suburb, went to work in an office, loved his wife and his son, and ate roast dinners with his parents every Sunday. Jacob was the only normal person in Louis' life. Everyone else had an agenda. He worried that even Felicity had an agenda. Why else would she refuse – twice – to marry him? What game was she playing? No one – absolutely no one – ever said *no* to the Prince of Wales.

Time was running out. If she didn't say *yes* sometime soon, then matters would be taken out of his hands, and goodness knew who would then be foisted on him. According to his mother – whose rule was law within the family, if not quite so much in the country – he was going to be married before the year was out whether he liked it or not.

Well, he didn't like it – not one little bit – but he'd made one too many shows of himself in public to take the moral high-ground with her. And, of course, there was the *other thing*. The *thing* he wasn't allowed to talk about. That pretty much scuppered any argument he might have had.

Marriages within the royal family didn't tend to be successful. His parents didn't have a happy union. He'd grown up listening to their heated arguments and had to bear witness to the pain his father inflicted on his mother with his many affairs. His father's dogged belief in his right to sleep with as many women as he chose should've had a steadying effect on Louis. Instead, it threw him a curveball, and he was often ashamed to find that he was a chip off the old block.

Regardless of her own experience, the queen fervently believed that marriage would be the making of her son. If there had been time, she might have given him some wriggle-room to find the right woman, but there wasn't any time. He'd chosen Felicity, and she'd given her consent for him to pursue her, but on the proviso that – should he fail to persuade her – she would get to choose his bride.

The thought of marrying anyone other than Felicity made his head hurt.

It wasn't that he loved her. He didn't love any woman, except, benignly, his mother and his sister, and they didn't count. It was simply that she was the best out of a bad bunch. He felt rather guilty thinking that and wondered if that truly made him an ass. Jacob often called him an ass, and he shuddered to think what Patricia said about him behind his back. He was sure that it was all well-deserved, and – now that his hangover was forcing him to be honest with himself – he didn't blame Felicity one little bit for turning him down. He might be the Prince of Wales, but he wasn't exactly a catch.

Catch, or not, it didn't alter the fact that she had to marry him. He had to make her see that she didn't have a choice – just as *he* didn't have a choice. Of course, it would help if he stayed away from headline-creating situations. No woman wanted to see the man she was destined to marry cavorting with pretty blonde soap-stars or leggy models.

He was going to have to start to behave himself – at least until he was safely married.

The bedroom door creaked open, and a plate full of sandwiches preceded a hairy arm into the room.

Jacob appeared. He wasn't smiling. 'It's gone eleven. It's time you were up and out of here.'

'It's early, yet,' Louis groaned, flopping back against the pillows.

Jacob placed the sandwiches on the bed. 'I need you to leave, mate. Patricia will be ringing in a while, and – you know her – she has some sort of weird extra-sensory perception. She'll know that you're here.'

'Remind me again why you married that woman.'

'Because she's smarter than me.' He dragged apart the curtains and pushed open the window. 'She's so smart that she would never have you for a friend.'

'Charming.'

'But, sensible. You're a terrible friend, Louis. Goodness knows what sort of a husband you'll make.'

'A pretty naff one, I'm sure, but who'll care?'

'Your wife?'

'Hmmm.' He sat up and grabbed a sandwich. The grease dripped down his chin as he took a huge bite. 'I don't like bacon.'

'But you're eating it?'

'I have to do a lot of things I don't like. Eating bacon is the least of it.'

Jacob sighed. 'I don't feel sorry for you, so stop feeling sorry for yourself. You're your own worst enemy.'

'I know. I've promised myself that I'll behave.'

'I've heard that before.'

'She won't marry me if I carry on like this.'

'She won't marry you... *period*, Louis.'

He threw the half-eaten sandwich back onto the plate. 'What do you know about what she'll do?'

'I know Felicity. She has her head screwed on.'

'Ah, I forgot... you were there to witness her humiliation.'

'No, Louis... I was there to witness *you* being *you*. You messed her up once, and she's much too sensible to allow you to mess her up a second time.'

'We were just kids. She doesn't hold it against me.'

'You think?' Jacob shook his head and gave a bemused smile. 'Think what you like, mate, but don't be surprised if you get your third knock-back soon.'

'I'll charm a ring onto her finger... you just watch me.'

'You'll need more than charm. You'll need a whole lot of luck. Thankfully, you have her mother on-side. I suggest you lean on her to pull a few strings.'

'That might be counter-productive. Felicity doesn't listen to her mother. She knows she's in cahoots with *my* mother.'

Although Jacob said that he didn't feel sorry for Louis, he actually did. His friend had everything – good looks, money, prestige, intelligence, a sense of humour, and a bucketload of charisma – but he was an unhappy man at heart. He was surrounded by people, but Jacob believed that he was the loneliest man on the planet. He wouldn't swap places with him for a king's ransom.

'Coffee is in the kitchen when you're ready,' he said. 'Try and be gone when my wife phones.'

'Why don't you try standing up to her once in a while?' he said, kicking back the quilt and pulling himself into a sitting position. 'She'll respect you more.'

'My wife respects me well enough,' he returned. 'I just happen to realise what side of my bread is buttered.'

'Yeah? You go on believing that mate. Patricia is smart, right enough. She certainly knows how to play you.'

'You're getting pretty close to crossing a line, Louis.' Jacob frowned and shook his head. 'I'm beginning to wonder just what I see in you.'

Louis wondered that, too. He was a lousy friend. 'I'm sorry,' he said. 'All this marriage business is making me a jabbering idiot.'

'Then, *you* put your foot down. Tell your mother to take a hike.'

He sighed and dropped his head. 'That'll never happen.'

Chapter Two

It was quite absurd, and she was mightily fed up with the whole debacle. She sat pondering the situation and wondered – not for the first time – *why her*. For years, and - up until recently - she'd hardly spoken more than half a dozen words to him. They didn't frequent the same establishments, and they had few, if any, mutual friends, so when he sought her out, at first she was intrigued, and then she was angry.

She'd thought that he wanted to apologise to her. Ten years was a long time to not say *I'm sorry*. If he'd only said it – and meant it – she probably wouldn't hate him quite so much.

He hadn't wanted to apologise. It seemed it was the furthest thing from his mind. She'd avoided him the whole night but had often felt his eyes on her. When he'd finally cornered her, she'd mentally prepared herself to be gracious, and to accept his apology cordially.

The ridiculous thing was – he wanted to marry her. He'd come right out with a proposal, and she'd been absolutely astounded. At first, she thought he was drunk, and then she thought he'd done it as some childish dare. When she'd realised that he was being perfectly serious, she'd found the whole thing painfully funny.

Louis didn't appreciate being laughed at. That was one thing she remembered from the time before he broke her heart. He'd been sensitive back then, but she'd thought that – after ten years – he would've grown out of that.

Obviously not.

She couldn't help herself. She'd laughed him all the way out of the room.

And, then she'd stumbled to the toilet and cried.

The tears were very real, and very heartfelt. She'd dreamt of marrying him. For almost all of those ten long years, she'd carried the memory of their love in her heart, and then she'd woken up to herself, and realised that it had all been one-sided. He'd never loved her at all, and she'd allowed herself to slowly begin to hate him. Perhaps hate was too strong a word for how she'd grown to feel about him, because – after his proposal – she discovered that she had no real clue about what her true feelings were.

But marriage? It was quite absurd. If she'd agreed, it would've been the beginning of the torturous death of her soul. Marrying Louis was a mistake she was determined never to make. Her sanity was much too precious to risk on him. She knew what he was. No matter how much she wished it otherwise, she knew that he wasn't for her.

She'd hoped that was the end of the matter, but it seemed that Louis was determined to have her.

The second proposal came in a text – *a text, of all things.* She'd wondered who had given him her phone number, and what means he'd applied to wheedle it out of that person.

She'd replied immediately.

Perhaps threatening to jump off Tower Bridge rather than marry him was a bit extreme, but she'd almost meant it.

She could have borne the whole ridiculous situation if only her mother hadn't known. She wasn't surprised that she'd got wind of it. After all, her mother was bosom buddies with the queen. Her mother knowing of Louis' intentions made everything a little more complicated.

Why didn't anyone think as she did – that there was something fishy about a man proposing, out of the blue, to an old flame? That it was perfectly reasonable for the Prince of Wales to be in hot pursuit of someone he'd unceremoniously dumped ten years previously?

She sat for a moment, gripping the arm of the chair, and looked across the table at her friend.

Alice thought she was mad.

Everyone thought she was mad.

'How does *over my dead body* grab you?'

Alice gave a dramatic sigh. 'Oh, Felicity, you really do take the biscuit. Do you know how many of our friends would gladly give up their left kidney to marry him? You should consider his proposal a bit more seriously.'

One word played over and over in her mind – *never... never...*

'I mean,' she went on, 'He's definitely my idea of the perfect husband.'

Felicity looked at her in astonishment. 'You're kidding?'

Alice shrugged. 'Okay, perhaps not perfect, but you must admit he's quite the eyeful.'

'Surely, you wouldn't marry him?'

'I'd certainly give it some thought,' she said. 'I wouldn't just dismiss his proposal out of hand.'

'Then, it's a pity he didn't ask you instead of me.'

Alice thought about that. 'Why *did* he ask you? We've all asked ourselves that question.'

'Gossiping behind my back, Alice?'

'Only amongst friends, darling. You must admit – it's a deliciously intriguing riddle. Why did the magnificently handsome, playboy Prince of Wales, ask *you* to be his bride? No offence, Felicity, but you wouldn't exactly be my choice for our next queen.'

'Gee... thanks, Alice.'

She flapped a hand. 'It's not that you wouldn't be capable. It's that you're much too beautiful, and much too fragile.'

'Fragile?'

'Well, look how much of a state you got yourself into last time.'

'That was ten years ago.'

'That's what turned you fragile. We often say...'

'*We?*'

'Us... your friends.' Alice frowned. 'Don't be obtuse.'

'Sorry, it's just that I never thought I'd be your sole topic of gossip.'

'You're not, but – since this whole marriage proposal business came up – you're one of our top five most interesting friends.'

'So, you all think that him dumping me all those years ago has made me what... weak? A pushover?'

'Vulnerable may be a better word.'

'Vulnerable to what?'

'Everything, I suppose.'

'I'm not a weak person, Alice. I know how to stand up for myself.'

'Then, accept his proposal... marry him. What are you so scared of?'

Not being loved. Being hurt. Having her self-esteem destroyed for a second time. Being humiliated by his philandering. The list of what scared her was a long one.

'I'm not scared of anything,' she lied.

'Well, marry him then. *He* wants it. *The queen* wants it. Your *mother* wants it. There's no point in you swimming against the tide.' Alice sighed, reached out, and patted her friend's hand across the table. 'Forget about the past, Felicity. He was younger then. You were both still teenagers. He didn't know what he wanted.'

'He wasn't a teenager – he was twenty years old, and he knew *exactly* what he wanted.' She drew her hand away. 'The problem was – I wouldn't give it to him.'

'Then, more fool you.' It was obvious that Alice was losing patience with her friend. 'Everyone did it back then. Everyone does it now. For goodness' sake, you're twenty-eight already, and I bet you still haven't given it away. You're probably the oldest virgin I know.'

'Please, Alice... drop the subject.'

'You're such a prude.'

Felicity huffed in a breath. Calling her a prude was Alice's way of insulting her. She really didn't know why she kept her on as her best friend. Perhaps it was because – despite her penchant for throwing insults – she was terribly loyal, kind, and very generous.

'I can't marry someone I hate,' she said.

'Oh, there speaks someone without a clue. Don't you know that the royals always marry for convenience? I know, for a fact, that Louis' parents can't stand one another.'

'He's very like his father.'

'Who... Louis?' Alice nodded. 'You're not wrong there.'

'I can't marry someone who's going to cheat on me.'

'He might not.' Even Alice didn't believe her own words.

'Even so...'

'Nothing is ever guaranteed, Felicity. Men are fickle creatures.'

'I don't want a fickle man.'

Alice cocked a brow. 'You could do worse than Louis.'

'I doubt it.'

'Why don't you think about it?'

'No.'

'But...'

'Look...' A beat. 'I hate him, okay? It's as simple as that.' She took a quick swallow of coffee. 'If truth be told – I more than hate him.'

'How can you *more than* hate someone?'

'Well, you can hate someone, *and* have no respect for them.'

'Okay – I get that.'

'And you can hate them, not respect them, *and* not trust them.'

'Okay – I agree - I can see where trust would be an issue with him.'

Felicity nodded, satisfied that she'd managed to get her point across.

Alice eyed her shrewdly. 'They all have affairs. I've never known a married man who never fooled around.'

'That's an audacious thing to say. Did your father cheat on your mother?'

'No, but...'

'Well, then...'

'All I'm trying to say is that there's no point in you waiting around, and hanging onto your virginity, in the hope that you'll find a man who will be faithful to you. You might as well marry Louis because that man doesn't exist.'

'You're so cynical.'

'I'm a realist, Felicity, and it's about time you woke up and smelled the coffee. Anyway - your mother and the queen are as thick as thieves, and both determined to get you up that aisle. Neither you, nor Louis, stand a chance against either of them.'

'Well, I'm not having it. It will be over...'

'Your dead body. I know – you said already.'

Felicity's shoulders slumped. Alice was right – she didn't stand a snowball's chance in hell in going against the country's two most formidable women. Not for the first time, she thought about packing up and running away.

It was all so utterly crazy. It was the twenty-first century, and not the Middle Ages. No one could make her get married to someone she detested. They could persuade and cajole. They could threaten and bully, but they couldn't drag her kicking and screaming towards the alter. They couldn't force the words *I do* from between her lips.

Felicity caught a movement in the periphery of her eye. Where they were seated - just inside and to the left of the door – meant that there was a lot of foot traffic passing by on the way in and out of the café, but someone entering had stopped at their table. She looked up.

Louis! What the..?

Felicity wasn't usually a blusher. Her complexion was more likely to pale rather than flare with heat whenever she was embarrassed or caught unawares. However, the sight of the POW standing hovering over her like an avenging devil, not only caused her cheeks to burn, but she suddenly felt every nerve- ending across her body catch alight.

'Small world,' he drawled. 'Fancy bumping into you here.'

She knew it was deliberate. There was no way he just happened to wander into the small, nondescript café situated on the smallest backstreet in town.

Her mother must have told him where she usually lunched.

'Hello, Louis,' Alice said, squirming in her seat and blushing to the roots of her hair. 'What brings you to this droll little place?'

'You know me, Alice – I like to try new things, and I heard the coffee here is to die for.'

Felicity winced as her knee jerked and struck the underside of the table. She was suddenly a bag of nerves.

Louis looked down on her with a small smile on his face. 'Hello Felicity,' he said. 'Isn't this fortuitous?'

Felicity had no intention of speaking to him. She gave her throbbing knee a rub, scooted over, and got out from behind the table, doing her best not to brush against him as she stood. Her lunch hour was nearly up, and it was at least a ten-minute walk back to the office, so she had a genuine excuse to leave.

'You are going already?' Alice looked down at her watch. 'Is that the time?' She jumped up from her seat and grabbed her bag. 'I'm going to be late.'

'Was it something I said?' Louis' expression was suddenly deadpan. 'I don't usually have women fleeing at the sight of me.'

No, he was certainly right about that, Felicity thought bitterly. With his drop-dead-gorgeous eyes, his sexy designer stubble, and his perfectly proportioned body, women flocked to him, latched on, and often refused to let go.

She felt the heat return to her face. She dropped her eyes, embarrassed as she recalled how she'd tried to hold onto him when all he'd wanted to do was cast her off.

The memory of how she'd almost succumbed – had almost given in and surrendered herself to him – shamed her. She knew that, in the end, she would have, just to keep him, but – by then – it was too late.

He'd already moved on. She'd denied him her body, and ultimately lost him.

Most of the time she'd had no regrets. Over the years, he'd shown himself to be less than worthy of any woman's virginity, but that had never stopped her wondering what might have been. If she'd given herself to him, would he be a better man today? Would they still be together as a couple, and would they already be planning their wedding?

She didn't think so. He might have ended up breaking her completely.

'Nice to see you, Louis,' Alice said, reaching out to squeeze his arm. 'Oh, I see you still work-out. You have muscles on muscles.'

Put him down, Alice! 'I'll ring you later,' Felicity said to her, throwing her an unamused scowl.

Louis took a step back and watched as the two women air-kissed. He'd never understood that habit. As far as he was concerned, you should kiss someone properly – lips to lips, or lips to skin – or just leave it alone.

Felicity was a head taller than her friend, and her slender, almost willowy body, was in sharp contrast to Alice's more rounded, dumpier frame. Louis didn't have one type that he favoured over another. He liked most women's bodies, but he had to admit that Felicity had the edge over most. His one regret in life was that he'd never seen it in all its naked glory.

He hoped to remedy that pretty soon.

Felicity watched Alice go and then went to the counter to pay for both their lunches. She scrabbled about in the bottom of her bag for some loose change to make up the total amount owed and discovered that she didn't have enough. She'd have to use her credit card. It was nearly maxed-out, and the cost of both meals would take her over the limit.

'Let me pay,' he said behind her.

Was he still there?

'No need,' she said, without turning

'I insist.'

She looked over her shoulder in dismay. *What the hell was he playing at?*

There was a ghost of a smile at the corners of his mouth. He saw the full spectrum of emotions flit across her face and he suddenly grinned. 'It's okay... I know I'm the last person you want to see. You've been avoiding me like the plague for weeks.'

He reached into his wallet and extracted his gold card. He handed it over and the woman behind the counter who then placed it in the card reader.

'There's no need ...'

'I said... I insist.'

'I'll pay you back.'

'I'm sure you will.' His grin turned wolfish.

She shifted her gaze and gave a wan smile to the woman standing goggle-eyed watching them. The poor woman actually thought that Louis was God's gift.

If only she knew.

'Do you want a lift?'

She jerked her attention back to him. 'No, thanks. I'm happy to walk.'

'I'll walk with you.' He took her elbow and steered her away from the counter and towards the door. He ignored the dozens of eyes feasting on him from every side. 'It'll give us a chance to talk.'

Pulling her arm from his grasp, she said, 'We've got nothing to talk about.'

'Well, that's not strictly true, Felicity. We have a wedding to plan.'

'In your dreams.'

'Not only there, my darling.'

'Don't you *my darling* me,' she said, drawing her five-foot five-inch frame up to its full height. 'You won't fool me a second time Louis.

You're a royal rat, and I wouldn't marry you if my life depended on it, and the sooner that you and your mother get that into your heads, the better.'

She threw herself through the door and almost stumbled onto the road. His hand at her elbow steadied her.

'Won't you forgive me?' he asked, his face suddenly all puppy-dog cute. 'I'll be eternally sorry for how I ended things with you.'

'Oh, really? You're sorry?' she shook her head in disbelief. 'After ten years, you say you're sorry. Why should I believe your lies now? Is it because *mummy* insists that you win me over?'

His eyes clouded over, and she could have sworn she saw a flash of pain in them.

'No, Felicity – *mummy* has nothing to do with me trying to apologise, or for me trying to persuade you to marry me. She has no power to make me do anything.'

'Well, you've got that right. She hasn't managed to stop you sowing your wild oats in all the top houses in London, and she certainly hasn't wielded enough power to prevent you having your antics broadcast across social media. So, tell me – just what *game* are you playing?'

'No game. I'm deadly serious. I'm going to marry you, Felicity, and the sooner you accept that fact, the better.'

'You must have a screw loose... it's the only explanation.' She shook her head. 'I guess you've to be pitied, more than loathed.'

'You don't loathe me.'

'That just shows how little you know.'

'I know that you want me. You never stopped wanting me.'

'It was *not* wanting you that broke us up... remember?'

They were jostled closer together by the pedestrians pushing past them. He pulled her into the doorway of a boarded-up shop.

'We were just kids,' he said. 'I feel I need to apologise for my rampant hormones.'

'You were twenty, Louis... hardly a kid.'

'But I should've realised how young you were. I should've given you time. I know that, now.'

'What a load of...' She stepped back out onto the pavement. 'Good-bye, Louis. Stop stalking me, or I'm going to report you.' She made to move off but was stopped by him yanking on her arm.

'I'm not going to give up,' he said. 'You'd better get used to seeing me around every corner.'

He dipped his head and snatched a kiss before turning and walking back towards his car, parked on double-yellow lines on the kerb outside the café.

She saw his protection officer open the door for him and, as he disappeared into the back seat, she suddenly remembered to breathe.

Chapter Three

The room vibrated with her mother's heavy footsteps. She wasn't an overly large woman, but rooms always shook whenever she travelled over them. It was something that simply defied natural physics.

It was a beautiful room. Her mother called it the Grey Parlour. It was the only room in the huge town house that Felicity felt comfortable in – that, and her bedroom.

She sat on one of the plush sofas and prepared herself for her mother's criticism. Her mother was very good at laying censure on just thick enough to be noticed, but not too thick so as to be considered bitchy.

Felicity was well used to it, and usually accepted it with reasonable grace.

'I should slap your impertinent face, my girl. Do you know how humiliated I was when you said that to the queen?'

Felicity's eyes lost focus. *Not this again.* 'Said what, mum? I've already told you - she rang me, and I gave a simple answer to a simple question. I wasn't rude. I was very polite. I mean – who would be stupid enough to be rude to the queen?'

Elizabeth Smythe-Walters was a lady in her own right, and one of the queen's closest friends. She was a die-hard royalist and wanted nothing more than to see herself raised far above her peers by the marriage of her daughter to the Prince of Wales. She wasn't going to allow the simple fact that her daughter was dead set against it to scupper that fervent ambition.

Her body tensed and her face took on a stern expression. 'It might've been a simple question, Felicity, but there was no need to be quite so blunt in your reply. You could've at least said that you were considering it.'

'That would've been a lie. Surely, you didn't want me to lie to her?'

Felicity was becoming increasingly fed-up and frustrated with the continual bickering. It didn't help that her mother seemed to be stuck in some Victorian melodrama. Two women - who couldn't, or wouldn't, accept the times they lived in – were doing their level best to bully her into submission. She recognised her mother's motives, but – for the life of her – she couldn't understand why the queen wanted the marriage so badly.

'Of course, I didn't want you to lie to her. How could you imply such a thing? I just wanted you to use a little diplomacy.'

She looked up at her mother. 'I'm not a diplomat,' she returned on a sigh. 'I'm a legal secretary with no plans to marry any time soon. That's what I told the queen, and it's not my fault that you're upset with my decision.'

'Why?' she asked her. 'Why refuse him? You like him well enough, don't you?'

''No... I can't say that I do. I don't like him one little bit, and...' she went on, 'surely you ought to love the man you plan to marry?'

'Love can come later.'

'Like it did with you and dad?' She immediately regretted the words. 'I'm sorry, mum. I shouldn't have said that.'

'No, well... it's said, now. There's no taking it back.' She sniffed and sat herself down on the very edge of a chair. 'I only want what's best for you.'

Not for yourself, mother? Not to be the mother of the next queen? How grand that would make you.

'Marrying Louis wouldn't be what's best for me. I'd be miserable.'

She wasn't surprised that her mother wouldn't let it go. From the moment she'd been born, and shortly after she drew her first breath, her mother had begun to make plans for her one and only daughter. Over the years, those plans had culminated in a desire to see her married into the royal family, and Felicity had never been blind to the fact that she'd decided to settle for nothing less than her marriage to Louis.

At a young age, Felicity had learned of her mother's aspirations, and – not knowing any better – had allowed herself to be manipulated into situations where Louis would notice her.

And, notice her, he did.

It had been instilled in Felicity that her destiny was to be queen, and she'd often wondered if that was the main reason she'd been so devastated when Louis broke up with her.

No, she'd loved him. He broke her heart.

'I'll never marry him,' she said. 'Not ever.'

'Not ever?' Her mother made a noise in the back of her throat. 'We'll see.'

Felicity closed her eyes and groaned. *Was there to be no let up*?

'I'm not going to change my mind,' she said. 'So, will you please stop going on about it?'

'Only if you promise to apologise to the queen.'

'Apologise? For what?'

'Disappointing her Majesty.'

'Oh, please...' She ran a weary hand through her hair and shook her head. 'You're all stark, raving bonkers. The three of you – Louis included. You're all insane.'

The clock on the far wall chimed the hour, distracting them, and they both took a moment to breathe and to settle their thoughts.

Felicity wanted to call a truce. 'I'm sorry,' she said, quietly. 'I know how much this means to you.'

Her mother nodded, accepting the apology. She sighed. 'I know you loved him once... that's why I can't let it go.'

'I don't love him anymore, mother. You must remember the state I was in when he dumped me? You must remember how hurt I was?'

'This isn't a soap opera, Felicity. No one actually ever gets their heart broken.'

'Well, mine broke, all right. He saw to that.'

'Then, allow him to make amends.'

'By marrying me?' She let out an explosive laugh. 'You've got to be kidding?'

'You know very well that I don't make jokes, Felicity.' She dragged in a breath. 'I'm afraid that I will have to put my foot down.'

Uh, oh! Here comes the ultimatum.

'If you continue to refuse to marry him, then I hope you under-stand that things will never be the same between us.'

Felicity *did* understand. Her mother was always one for the dra-matic gesture. It seemed that – if she didn't toe the line and marry the POW – her mother would make a grand show of cutting her out of her life.

Well, she could live with that far easier than living as Louis' wife.

What if he promised to be faithful?

She could never trust that promise.

What if he truly loved her?

He loves no one but himself.

Leaving her mother sulking, she went immediately to her bedroom, dropped down onto her knees and searched for her special box.

It was nothing fancy – just a battered Quality Street tin – but she'd lined it with pink crepe paper and had placed a bar of Louis' favourite soap inside, so that, when she prised off the lid, she was hit with the fa-miliar scent of green apple.

She didn't torture herself very often. These days, opening the box, was a rare occurrence.

Her fingers brushed aside the tiny bouquet of paper roses he'd made her and found the strip of photo-booth pictures. There were four in the strip and, in each of them, she looked deliriously happy snuggled against his chest, her head resting beneath his chin. Unlike their friends having similar snaps taken, they didn't make funny faces, or acted like clowns. They'd both wanted a serious memory of the day.

They'd snatched a kiss in one of them, and – in the final one – they'd simply stared into one another's eyes. Anyone looking at those photographs would see love... wouldn't they? She hadn't been wrong about how they'd both felt about one another. Those snaps were her proof.

Several times over the years, she'd come close to taking a pair of scissors to them, but something had always stopped her from destroying the memory of that day. Looking at them, she could almost believe that he'd truly loved her. She'd certainly loved him.

There was a single Valentine's card. He'd not sent it anonymously, preferring to add a personal message and to sign it.

My dearest, darling Valentine. You make me whole. I love you. Yours forever, Louis.

She'd received the card three days before he told her it was over between them.

So much for *Yours forever.*

Her memories of the days and weeks after the *bombshell dumping* still made her feel terribly embarrassed. She couldn't believe she'd been *that* girl – the girl who begs for a second chance, who ejects her pride into the stratosphere, and who resorts to stalking in order to never have the man she loved out of her sight for a moment. But, she *had* been that girl – with bells on.

She cringed just thinking about it.

Thankfully, she'd come to her senses before she had rung him up and proposed a rendezvous that would include sex. Well – if truth be told – she hadn't really come to her senses in time. Ultimately, her virginity had been saved because Louis had found himself someone else.

In typical Louis fashion, he had no idea how much he'd devastated her. He had been far too self-centred to notice. That turned out to be a blessing because she never had to suffer him looking at her with pity in his eyes. She could be in his company, join him with their other university friends at parties and other social events, and all without the merest hint of an atmosphere between them.

She had always been proud of herself for – after her initial broken-hearted madness – acting as if she didn't give a shit. Then, with time moving on, the occasions when they'd be in the same room grew fewer and fewer until the only time she caught sight of him was on the television, in the newspapers, or on social media posts.

That was why the encounter at her friend's birthday party had come as such a shock. Never, in her wildest dreams, could she have imagined that the only reason he was there was because of her.

She closed the lid on the box and pushed it back under the bed. She thought she might get rid of it in the morning – throw it in the dustbin amongst the other rubbish.

It was time to let him go. Her future had to be a Louis-free one. There was no point in refusing to marry him, and then keeping that damned box.

No point at all.

Chapter Four

Louis held the crystal glass steady in his hand and sipped at the mellow cognac. He was churning with anger, but you would never know it to look at him. Even as a child, no one saw beneath the surface of his calm and nonchalant demeanour. He was a master of deception. He'd had to be, or he wouldn't have survived the rigour of royal life. He thought that – if his life had taken another course – he would've made a fine actor.

Whenever people – even those closest to him – looked at him, they all read something different in his eyes, or in his expression. Louis was described in a variety of ways. Some thought him aloof and unapproachable, some found him gregarious and generous, and some believed him to be nothing more than an overprivileged oaf. It would be impossible to find a single person who professed to really know what made him tick.

His mother – the queen – knew him least of all. That wasn't entirely due to the fact that he'd been raised by a succession of nannies, or that, growing up, he only ever saw her for a few minutes each day. She didn't know him because she'd never taken the time to try.

Whenever he was being introspective, Louis would contemplate the possibility that he couldn't relax into a relationship with the opposite sex enough to settle down because of his experiences in his formative years. The only constant female in his life had been his sister. There had been too many nannies, and too many missed hours with his mother, to truly know how to genuinely interact normally and not simply sexually with women. The lack of female companionship as a child took its toll, and – whenever he was being honest with himself – he acknowledged that there was something missing in his psyche, and he

25

wondered how fair it would be to inflict himself permanently on any single woman – particularly Felicity.

In public, the queen was the epitome of cordiality. She never – by a flash of her eyes, or a thinning of her lips – showed what she was really thinking. In the privacy of her own sitting room - behind closed doors, and with the servants out of earshot - his mother showed her true colours.

He drained the glass and attempted to filter out the drone of her voice. She'd been going on about how disappointed she was in him. He'd listened to over twenty minutes of complaints before closing down and allowing her words to wash over him.

He'd heard it all before, and he'd learned the hard way not to take her words to heart, but her put-downs remained difficult and onerous experiences.

Her voice – raised to a pitch that broke through his reverie – brought his attention fully back on her.

'You're not trying hard enough,' she said. 'You don't seem to be taking this seriously.'

He looked at her with cold grey eyes. He never looked at her with any warmth - not even now, when he knew that she was dying. Her terminal condition *had* shifted something in him, and he had tried to change his ways a little so as not to invoke so much ire from her, but it was too difficult to please her.

He'd sworn to himself that – should he ever have any children – he would love them with every fibre of his being. He wouldn't be critical, or cruel, or indifferent. No child of his would be neglected to such an extent that they feared of never being truly loved or wanted.

'I'm taking it as seriously as it warrants,' he said. 'But we can't force her to marry me. If you'd allow me to confide in her, to...'

'No.' The queen raised an imperial hand and glowered across the room at him. 'No one is to know until after this whole sordid affair is sorted.'

'I'd hardly call it sordid, mother.'

'What would you call it, then?'

'Unfortunate.'

She picked up a very expensive Tiffany vase and launched it at him. It missed his head by mere inches.

He didn't flinch. He knew how poor her aim was.

'Unfortunate? The Prime Minister wants to turn us into a republic, and you call it unfortunate?' She gave a bitter laugh. 'That's the understatement of the century.'

''He's simply full of hot air. I don't know why you're even giving his words any consideration.'

'Because he's the *Prime Minister*.'

'And you're the queen. Prime Ministers come and go, but you're the one constant, mother.'

'Not if he has his way.'

'Who is to say that he will?'

'I can't take the risk. It would be different if... if I wasn't so sick.'

He didn't want to think of her being sick, or what it meant for him and the country.

'It's all your fault. You were the last straw.'

His shoulders slumped under the weight of the blame she cast on him, but his gaze remained unaffected.

'My father should take most of the blame, not me. *He* ruined the monarchy. I'm merely your convenient scape-goat.'

'The apple doesn't fall far from the tree, does it?' She was panting with suppressed rage. 'You only have to pick up a newspaper to see how much you're your father's son.'

It was the same old story, and he was becoming mightily sick of hearing it.

'Against my better judgement, I agreed to your plan,' he said. 'I've been taking it all *very* seriously, because – despite what you might think, mother – I *do* recognise the importance of marrying. I know, full well, how much a royal wedding will bring the whole country behind us. If we pull it off, you can die knowing that your dynasty is secure.'

'Then, bring her on board. Get her to say *yes* and be done with it... or choose someone else. We're running out of time.'

'Well, she has to *want* me, first.'

'You never seem to have a shortage of women *wanting* you, Louis. Why is this one so different?'

He knew why. He'd hurt her in the past, and she obviously wasn't the forgiving type.

He couldn't really determine why he'd chosen Felicity to be his wife. Years ago, when he'd dated her, although he'd liked her well enough, he hadn't considered her all that special. He remembered her as being too clingy. She'd wanted something from him that he was incapable of giving, and the only thing he'd really wanted from her, she'd refused to relinquish. Their fledgling relationship had been doomed almost from the start, and he'd allowed it to end badly, so he wasn't surprised that she'd held a grudge, but – to refuse him now? What was that all about?

Perhaps he'd broken her heart?

'I mean it, Louis – if you can't seal the deal with Felicity, I'll find someone willing.'

It was typical of his mother to narrow the important decision of who was to be his wife, and the next queen, down to a mere *deal*. She still lived in the middle-ages. She still believed it was a perfectly reasonable state of affairs to barter and to manipulate two people into marriage.

He knew the sort of woman she would choose for him, and there was no way he wanted to be married to a Stepford wife. Felicity had gumption. He hadn't deliberately kept tabs on her over the years, but he'd come to know her as the woman, as opposed to the girl he'd once dated. He'd liked what he'd learned about the more mature Felicity.

Anyway, he thought that he owed her. If he had to marry someone, let it be someone he'd wronged, and someone who would be grateful enough not to hold him too much to account, but, yet still be feisty enough to give him a run for his money.

That woman was Felicity. He had no doubt about that – especially now that she was making him work to win her over. There was something incredibly sexy about the chase. He knew he wouldn't feel quite so sure in his choice if she'd simply rolled over and said *yes* at the first asking.

'Invite her to my birthday dinner next week. Let her see what she'd be missing if she continues to refuse you.'

Attending the dinner would be more likely to put her off even further, but – if his mother turned on the charm – he just might persuade her to give his proposal some serious consideration.

'If you spend the next few days romancing her, we might be able to announce the engagement at the dinner. Wouldn't that be perfect?'

'A bit ambitious,' he said, bending to pick up the pieces of the shattered lamp. 'It'll take more than a few days of romancing her to get her to agree.'

'I told you... we're running out of time.'

He placed the shards of porcelain on a small occasional table. 'I thought the doctors said you had at least another year?' Unbidden, he felt a twinge of sorrow. Regardless of everything, she *was* his mother.

'I meant about the Prime Minister. He doesn't know that I'm privy to his plans, and he's set to place a Bill before the Commons next month.'

'A Bill? How did he sneak that through the White Paper stage?'

'Some ancient ministerial prerogative... or some such nonsense.'

'The cheeky...'

'So, you see the urgency?'

He nodded. If he thought that the country would be better off as a republic, he would be the first to surrender to the inevitable, but he happened to believe that the monarchy did some good. His charities alone brought some level of prosperity to the needy, and the tourism generated by having a royal family, made up a hefty portion of the whole country's income.

He was more than willing to sacrifice himself to keep the royal dynasty alive. What he wasn't quite so sure about was whether he was prepared to sacrifice Felicity.

But needs must. He didn't have a choice – not if he didn't want to be burdened with some blue-stockinged choice of his mother.

'I'll see what I can do, mother. I'll give it my best shot.'

'See that you do, my boy. I refuse to die knowing that you destroyed centuries of this country being a sovereign state.'

He was trapped – trapped by her imminent death and trapped by his genuine wish to give her what she most wanted. He would be married before his mother died – of that there was no doubt – and he silently prayed that it would be to Felicity.

He was dismissed and made his way from the private sitting room to his office. There was a state visit planned to South Africa later in the year, and his mother hoped he would be able to combine it with his honeymoon. The plans for the visit were almost finalised and because there was an element of flexibility, he knew that incorporating a bride into the itinerary wouldn't be a problem.

His private secretary was waiting with a pile of papers for him to sign. The hum-drum business of his royal role was now going to keep him occupied for the remainder of the day, but he planned to spend the evening with Felicity. She didn't know it yet, but she was going out to dinner with him. He wanted them to be seen in public, on a date, and very much a couple. He was ready to begin the proper charm offensive and, by the time his mother's birthday dinner came around, she would be putty in his hands.

But, first, he had to discover the next convenient place to *accidentally* bump into her.

He rang Alice.

Chapter Five

When she read the invitation, Felicity felt something rise in her chest. It felt like the flutter of a giant butterfly with barbs on its wings. She tugged at the neck of her blouse and tried to drag air down into her lungs.

How dare he do this to me. How dare he pursue me when he knows my answer.

The invitation had arrived by special messenger a few moments earlier and, before she'd even opened it, she knew it was from *him*.

The words danced before her eyes, and something akin to panic assailed her. A feeling of dread slipped across her mind and caused her heart to thud against her ribs. She knew he wasn't going to give up, and the dread was brought about by the fact that she was already beginning to doubt her motives for refusing him.

She said it was because she hated him, because of his track-record of breaking women's' hearts, and for the fact that she knew she could never trust him. All of those reasons still stood true, but they weren't the only reasons. They weren't the true motivation for refusing him. If possible, the truth was much more tangible, and it was a truth she barely admitted - not even to herself.

Pushing the thought away before it clarified in her mind and forced her to face the truth, she slipped the card back inside the envelope, and placed a hand on the hall table to steady herself.

She lost the battle to gain control of herself and staggered back, feeling for the chair she knew was somewhere behind her.

I don't love him. I don't... I don't... I don't.

But she truly did. Seeing him in the café the day before, huffing in the scent of his skin, and finding her body react to his voice, had awakened in her a long-suppressed hunger. It wasn't lust, and it wasn't misconceived hate. It was love – pure and simple – and it hurt like hell.

Her thoughts raced. If she accepted, it would be tantamount to agreeing to marry him, and that was the last thing she wanted. It was bad enough that her mother thought it was a done-deal, without the whole country jumping on the band-wagon – which they would do if she arrived at the birthday dinner on his arm.

What would be so wrong with that? You love him, so why not marry him? Because of all the reasons that plagued her. She knew that it was more than possible to hate someone just as much – if not more – than you loved them. She had the proof of it stabbing and jabbing away at her through every waking moment.

If she had no pride, and no expectation of being loved back, she would marry him like a shot.

But he would hurt her again. She had no doubt about that. He would end up destroying her, and she had too much self-worth to permit that to happen. She would not be humiliated. She would not marry him simply to be a broodmare, and she would not, *repeat not*, attend his mother's stupid birthday dinner.

'What are you doing?' Her mother's voice spiked through her brain, interrupted, and put paid, to her almost full-blown panic attack.

'Nothing.'

'What's that in your hand? Has the post arrived already?' She glanced at her watch. 'It's only just gone ten.'

'No, the post hasn't arrived,' she returned, standing up and folding the envelope into a tight little square which she held flat against her palm.

'It was a courier, wasn't it? He brought something from Louis?'

She wanted to shake her head. She wanted to deny it, but she didn't want to lie. She wouldn't have him making her lie.

'It's an invitation,' she said. 'To the queen's rather intimate birthday dinner. I'm not going.'

There was a long pause, during which Felicity saw her mother's eyes narrow, and her lips thin.

There was going to be fireworks.

'I mean it, mother – I'm not going. It was unfair of him to invite me.'

'There's nothing *fair* about any of this,' she snapped, her voice a cold slap. 'What's *fair* about turning down a perfectly, well-meaning proposal of marriage without a single, justifiable reason?'

'I *have* reasons,' she snapped right back at her. 'And, what's well-meaning about him wanting someone just to have babies?'

'Who mentioned anything about babies, for goodness' sake?'

'Why else would he be so anxious for a wife? The queen obviously wants a grandchild. She's desperate for Louis to have an heir, and I'm the convenient womb to provide it.'

She'd embarrassed her mother with talk of wombs. She was terribly conservative, and exceptionally prudish, and Felicity should have known better than to even hint at the sex act. She might not have actually said it, but even her mother knew what it took to plant a baby in a woman's womb.

'I'm sorry,' she said. 'But it's the truth.'

'That boy has feelings for you. You can't deny that.'

'That *boy* is a man who has feelings for a great many women, mother. I wouldn't dream of imagining that I meant any more to him than any of the others.'

'I'm sure he'd give them all up once he married you.' Her shoulders sagged. 'I wish you'd be a little more mature about all of this.'

She envisioned simply walking away. She could go upstairs, pack a suitcase, and leave. She had time owing from work and could easily afford to take a month off. That would get her past the birthday bash, and a few weeks left over for Louis to attach his attention elsewhere for a bride.

Her mother was talking at her again. She could see her lips move, but she'd already shut the sound out. She'd heard enough. If she heard any more about the POW, she would scream.

She swallowed back hard. She knew that she wouldn't run away. After he cruelly dumped her, Louis had turned her into a recluse, and her self-imposed withdrawal from her friends and her life had lasted many long months. She wouldn't allow him to do that to her again.

On a sudden impulse, she said, 'I'll go to the dinner, mother.' Her mother's eyes widened a fraction. 'But I'll attend as a private individual, and not as his personal guest.'

Felicity could see her mother's brain working behind her eyes. It was obvious she was trying to work out if that would be an acceptable compromise.

'Very well, but – if he asks you to dance – I expect you to accept.'

'There will be dancing?'

'Well, it's a party, and not simply a dinner. Of course, there will be dancing.'

'Are you going?'

'Of course,' she sniffed. 'The queen personally invited me.'

Felicity dipped her head, already regretting her hasty decision.

'You'll require a new dress.'

'I don't think so. I'm not spending my hard-earned wages on a dress I'll probably never wear again.'

'I'll pay for it.'

'*You'll* pay?' She couldn't remember the last time her mother had bought her anything. Her last few birthdays had gone by without even a card. They weren't exactly a rich family. Yes, her mother was from an old, aristocratic line of Lords and ladies, and, yes, they lived in a huge house, and her mother was a friend of the queen, but money was tight.

Or perhaps it's just your mother who's tight?

'There's no need to spend money on a dress for me,' she returned. 'I have the perfect dress in mind, and it's already in my wardrobe.' She was thinking of the black Victoria Beckham number she'd never worn. Okay, she'd bought it second-hand from an exclusive dress agency, but it was certainly worthy of wearing to a formal dinner – a royal birthday party notwithstanding.

'Nonsense. It's a special occasion, and I'm sure that nothing you own that will possibly be good enough.'

Why didn't that statement surprise her? Nothing about her was ever good enough for her mother.

'Whatever,' she sighed. 'It's your money.'

'It's settled, then.' She eyed the folded card held tight in Felicity's fist. 'You'll reply right away?'

She nodded, not daring to say another word in case she said something she *really* regretted.

Satisfied, her mother walked from the hall and through into the large drawing room that overlooked the street.

Felicity actually hated living in the house that had been in her mother's family for generations. She wished that she lived with her father – a banker who resided in New York. Her parents weren't divorced – heaven forbid that there was ever a divorce in the family – but they'd lived apart since Felicity was a child.

Although she only saw her father once or twice a year, she felt that he knew and understood her far better than her mother. He always paid attention to what she had to say, and she couldn't recall a time when he'd been in the least critical of the choices she made. She'd missed him terribly when he left, but – even at such a young age – she understood his reasons. Her mother wasn't the easiest person to be married to. She'd always appeared to be resentful of her husband's less than prestigious bloodline and had always been constantly looking down her nose at him. Their relationship was never going to be conducive to matrimonial bliss, and the house seemed to breathe easier once they'd officially separated.

Felicity had often wondered why her mother ever agreed to marry him. It wasn't as if they had anything in common, and they certainly hadn't moved in the same circles. Quite by chance, she discovered that her maternal grandfather had lost out big-time on the stock exchange, and an injection of money was required to keep them afloat. Her father had been the perfect solution. He was a self-made man, much smarter when it came to playing the market, and – being a romantic at heart – he really wanted to rescue the damsel in distress.

Her mother – a damsel? It didn't take her father long to realise his mistake. Apparently, his only stipulation for entering into a marriage of convenience was that he was given a child.

Felicity had been that child, and her mother had resented her from the minute she was born. As far as her mother was concerned, she'd been coerced into having her, but that didn't mean she had to like what she'd given birth to. She hadn't begun to pay attention to her only child until the moment she'd realised what an asset she was.

Blonde, beautiful, intelligent, and alluring – Felicity was going to be Lady Elizabeth Smythe-Walters' ticket to the big league. She didn't care about foisting an unhappy marriage onto her daughter, not so long as it paid dividends, and Felicity was astute enough to realise that. She knew that she would find it difficult to stick to her guns in the face of her mother's determination to see the marriage come about, but she knew that she could always look to her father for support. If needs be, she knew that he'd drop everything and fly to her side.

She would ring him – get his opinion on the situation. He was easy to talk to, easy to confide in, and she hoped that - - even thousands of miles away - he would be able to intervene and get her mother off her back.

Chapter Six

'Fancy meeting you here.'

Felicity turned on her heel and felt her ankle buckle. She almost went over, but he grabbed her elbow and hauled her upright. That was the second time in the past few days that he'd prevented her from crashing to the ground and, far from being grateful, she was furious.

Shaking her arm free, she backed up, and hissed, 'Are you stalking me?'

Louis feigned a look of shock. '*Me*... stalk *you*..?' He shook his head. 'No way, Felicity, but I might ask you that same question.'

'What?' she asked dumbly. 'You think..?'

'No. No... I'm joking. Lighten up, why don't you?'

She clenched her jaw so tightly that she feared she'd break her teeth. He was so infuriating. He'd only been back in the orbit of her life for a few short weeks, and she was already experiencing a whole myriad of unfamiliar emotions. She couldn't remember the last time a person made her feel so angry. Not even her mother, at her worst, could get the same rise out of her.

He *was* stalking her. She was in no doubt about that. First the café, and now her local supermarket – and that wasn't counting the times she'd seen him in the distance or caught sight of his car on the street outside her home.

Her mind screamed at him to leave her alone... be satisfied with having her attend his mother's dinner... give up on her and any hopes of marrying her.

'Would you believe me if I told you I simply popped in here to buy some razors?'

She shocked herself when she realised she had retained the ability to speak. 'No. You have flunkies to do your shopping.'

'Ah, yes... you got me there.' He had the good grace to appear sheepish. 'What if I said I came in here to use the toilet?'

'I'd say that you were a liar.'

He put his arms up in surrender. 'Okay – I *am* stalking you, but I have a good reason.'

'I doubt that.' She felt her anger dissipate. He wasn't worth that depth of emotion. 'You're just a sick individual.'

'Ouch.' He put a hand across his chest. 'You certainly know how to wound a man.'

'Well, you obviously have no concern about how you're wounding me, so you can't really complain, can you?'

He wanted to come back at her with something really pithy, but his mind went blank. He knew he shouldn't have shocked her by just appearing behind her - in a supermarket of all places – and he wasn't surprised at how angry she was.

Alice had given him the heads-up about Felicity's early Thursday evening routine of shopping in that particular supermarket. He'd hung out in the car park for nearly an hour before he'd spotted her mini arrive. Now, he wondered if his impromptu collision with her had been such a good idea. It was obvious that she hated surprises.

'I'm sorry,' he said. 'I can completely understand why you don't want me around. I'm an arse. I can't help being an arse. I try not to be, but I continually fail. Please forgive me.'

Her mouth twitched. She wanted to smile, but she knew she'd disgust herself if she did. It's what he wanted. If she smiled, he would believe he'd won some wonderful prize.

'Do you forgive me?'

'No. Not unless you promise to stay away from me until the dinner, and then get right out of my life afterwards.'

'Oh, Felicity, I really wish I could promise you that, but...'

'But, what? What's so difficult about that, Louis?'

He stared at her, his eyes almost filling his face. He had no idea how to answer her.

'Well?' She leaned against the shopping trolley and kept a tight hold of her irate expression. 'Are you going to explain all this madness to me? I mean – come on, Louis – I'm not exactly God's gift, am I? So, why chase after me like some love-sick puppy? Why torment me with marriage proposal after marriage proposal, and why act like a lunatic stalker?'

He knew he had to give her something. Any explanation was better than none. Whatever he said, he realised that it had to be as close to the truth as possible, or she would see right through him.

'I have to get married. My mother insists.' He gave a wan smile. 'I know how that sounds, and I'm almost embarrassed saying it, but it happens to be true, and there's nothing I can do but obey her direct command.' He huffed in a breath. 'She wants to choose some mousy little creature for me. She wants to foist some brainless airhead, with no backbone and without a single thought in her head to call her own, on me, but I put my foot down. I told her it was you, or no one.'

'That still doesn't explain why you want me.'

'Because you're sensible.'

Of all the things he could've said – that she was beautiful, desirable, his ideal woman – he had to plump for *sensible*. He saw her face fall and wished he could cut his tongue out. 'I didn't mean...'

She raised a hand. 'If I were you, I'd quit whilst I was ahead.'

'I should have said,' he went on, ignoring the hand, 'that I would feel comfortable with you as my wife.'

'The hole is getting deeper,' she said flatly. 'Perhaps you should stop digging.'

Pulling her cardigan around her, and huddling inside its woolly shield, she lowered her head and wished him gone. His presence, his words, his intentions, confused her.

'I'm usually pretty good with words,' he said, rather gently. 'But I can see I'm making a very poor show of explaining myself. I wish...' He shook his head – exasperated with himself. 'I wish we could start all over again.'

'Go back ten years, you mean?'

'No, not exactly.'

'Then, what would be the point?'

'I could've made that first proposal more romantic, I suppose.' He gave a rueful smile, remembering the first time he'd asked her to marry him.

He'd purposefully inveigled an invitation to one of her friend's birthday parties and, fortified with a glass or two of wine, had – although she'd made an effort to avoid him – cornered her, and simply blurted out that he wanted to marry her.

She'd laughed in his face and told him, in no uncertain terms, that he was the last man she'd ever consider marrying. He saw that she'd meant it, but that hadn't stopped him pursuing her. In fact, her refusal had had the effect of galvanising him. Stalking her had almost become a game to him.

Proposing the second time by text hadn't been one of his finer moments and he hoped that a candle-lit dinner and soft music would do the trick.

'Will you allow me to try again?'

'You mean – will I stand back and listen to yet another proposal?'

'No, not exactly. I'd like you to come out to dinner with me... just the two of us. If I can't persuade you to marry me this time, then I promise to leave you alone.'

He didn't mean it, but she wasn't to know that.

She greeted his words with silence. Part of her wanted to abandon her trolley and flee the supermarket, but another part – the part that hungered for him – told her to agree.

She didn't know what to say. The invitation to dinner had come as a complete shock and had left her too confused to think straight.

'I don't know,' she finally dragged out. 'I don't want to give you any false hope.'

'I promise not to hope.'

She saw the expression in his eyes and knew that was a lie.

'Okay,' she said, immediately regretting it. 'When?'

'Tonight.' He picked up a frozen ready meal from her trolley. 'It will save you having to microwave this rubbish.'

'Not tonight,' she replied, taking the package out of his hand, and tossing it back in the trolley. 'Perhaps after your mother's dinner?'

'No... it has to be tonight.'

'No, Louis – it doesn't.'

'Pretty please?'

She couldn't resist those eyes and – despite her better judgement – she finally agreed.

He was cock-a-hoop. As he watched her push her trolley towards the check-out – the microwave meal having been put back in the freezer – he began to believe that he was reaching the finish line with her. He'd promised not to hope, but there was no way he could prevent the excitement from bubbling all the way up from his toes.

She was going to say *yes* – he was sure of it.

Felicity put her shopping in the boot of the mini and climbed in behind the wheel. She'd felt his eyes on her all the way across the car park and had self-consciously tried not to wobble on her heels.

She'd said yes to dinner with him but was still adamant that she would never give him a yes to marriage.

Then, why did you agree to go out on a date with him? How bonkers are you?

They were reasonable questions – questions she had no answers to.

As she headed home, the only thought remaining in her head was – *what am I going to wear?*

Chapter Seven

The ready meal had been because Felicity's mother was out to dinner, and Felicity hadn't planned on keeping the cook late just for her. Now, they both had plans and, although Felicity knew where her mother was dining, and with whom, her mother had no idea of Felicity's plans, and she had no intention of telling her. She only hoped that Louis wouldn't confide in his mother, or the grapevine would soon put her mother straight.

She didn't ask herself what had possessed her to agree to the date. She didn't ask because she knew.

Some of what Louis said in the supermarket resonated with her. She'd found herself feeling sorry for him, and the predicament his mother had placed him in. She didn't quite buy the whole idea that his duty as POW somehow compelled him into marriage, but she had got the sense that there was something he wasn't telling her – something that had forced his hand.

She was determined to uncover what that *something* was.

She waited until her mother left before getting ready. She showered quickly and swept her hair back into a messy bun. The dress she chose was midnight blue and it flattered her curves and emphasised her long legs. She worried that she looked a little too sexy, and that she would give off the wrong impression, but she thought better of it. She wasn't going to hide herself behind an oversized sweater and a grungy pair of jeans just to save her blushes, or Louis any embarrassment. She knew she looked good, and there was nothing wrong in flaunting it.

He sent a driver for her. She expected that the car would head for one of the fashionable restaurants in town – perhaps *Circolo Popolare*, or *Hicce*, but it avoided all the routes that would take her to the types of places she knew that Louis frequented and headed, instead, to Westminster and then to Buckingham Palace.

Her heart was in her throat. Although her mother was a frequent visitor at the palace, Felicity had never been. She hoped that the car was merely making a detour to pick up Louis because, if she was to dine in his apartment, she didn't think she would be able to eat a thing.

The car pulled through the gates and drew to a halt. She sat, immobile, hoping to see Louis stride down the steps towards the car, and jerked in her seat when the door was dragged open.

There was no Louis – just the driver beckoning her out.

Goosebumps erupted the length and breadth of her body. She was really doing it – she was really just about to enter the palace to have dinner with the heir to the throne. She was too terrified to be excited.

A pit opened up in her stomach. She began to question the sensibility of agreeing to meet with him, and – despite the luxuriousness of the setting - she suddenly wished that she'd settled on the oversized sweater and the grungy jeans. There wouldn't be anyone else around to take the attention away from how her body looked in her dress. There would just be the two of them, and – with the way she looked – he would *definitely* jump to the wrong conclusion. She dreaded his eyes popping out of his head when he saw her.

There were no words to describe the grand staircase. Its dramatic scrolling balustrade was utterly breath-taking, and – what made it all the more spectacular – was her lithe prince holding onto the golden banister as he descended the plush red carpeted stairs.

He had a hint of a smile on his face, but her eyes didn't stay there. They travelled the length of him. Dressed in slate grey jeans, and a navy turtleneck sweater, he'd dressed down for the occasion, and she felt herself blush at the obvious contrast in their appearance. She felt immediately on the back foot. The effort she'd taken – thinking they would be dining in a sophisticated eatery – now seemed completely inappropriate.

He would think her a fool or – worse – a brazen hussy.

Louis' hand gripped the banister so tightly that his knuckles turned white. He found that he couldn't breathe. As his eyes drank her in, his smile wavered, and his heart almost burst from his chest.

Ravishing was not the word. She was completely, and utterly, stunning.

'You look...'

'I'm sorry.' She felt her whole body tremble. 'I thought we were eating out.'

'Gorgeous,' he finished. 'You look absolutely beautiful.'

He was directly in front of her. She had to crane her neck a little to look directly into his face. 'Thank you, but I'm a little bit overdressed.'

'For dinner at Bucks House?' His smile returned, stronger. 'I think that dress is just perfect.' He took her hand and raised it to his lips. 'Welcome to my home.'

The skin beneath his lips felt scorched.

His face shone with pride as he watched her eyes take in her surroundings. This could all be hers, he thought. If she agreed to be his wife, she would have the run of the place. There had been method in the madness of bringing her to the palace ahead of his mother's dinner party. She had to see for herself what she would be giving up if she continued to refuse him.

'This way,' he said, placing a warm hand on the small of her back and escorting her upstairs. 'I hope you're hungry. I've had chef prepare a feast for us.'

He led her to the second floor, and along the east wing to his suite of rooms. They were met by two liveried footmen – one holding a gilded tray with champagne flutes sitting prettily on it and bubbling with frothy wine – and it took every bit of inner strength to keep Felicity standing. Such was her awe, and such was her anxiety, that she feared that her legs would buckle.

She allowed her eyes to wander around the sitting room. It wasn't what she'd expected. She'd imagined fine antiques, priceless paintings, brocade chairs, and crystal – lots of crystal, but the room was rather plain, and surprisingly untidy.

Across the wide expanse of grey carpet, a door stood open at the far end of the room. She couldn't help but see a glimpse of his bed. As she imagined herself sprawled across it, an involuntary flush spread up from her neck and across her face. She twisted the stem of her glass and raised it to her lips. She hoped that a sip of the champagne would steady her.

It didn't.

Louis sensed her tension and immediately began to chatter about nothing in particular. He tried to make her laugh by telling her silly stories about what antics he got up to in the palace as a child. By the time they were seated at the small table in the window he was relieved to see that the colour in her cheeks had returned to almost normal.

'Are you all right?' he asked. 'Warm enough in that dress?' His eyes crinkled at the corners. 'You look hot enough to sizzle, but there's no heating in here... mother doesn't approve of wasting money on such a basic necessity as warmth – not in our private quarters, anyway.'

'I'm fine, thanks,' she said, her voice hollow, then belied her words with a shiver. She truly wasn't cold. It was a mixture of anxiety and dread that caused her body to tremble.

'I've shocked you... having you brought here,' he said. 'I'm sorry for not telling you. I wanted it to be a surprise.'

'Well – take it from me, Louis – I'm most definitely surprised.'

'A nice surprise?' He amazed himself at just how much he wanted her to be pleased.

She nodded and forced a smile. 'Definitely.'

He tried not to let his relief show. It could have all gone so horribly wrong. She might have bolted. She might have insisted that they go out to a restaurant.

'I wish you'd relax.'

'I *am* relaxed.' She dropped her shoulders from around her ears. 'See?'

He smiled. 'That doesn't cut it. You're all pent-up and as stiff as a board.' He reached out a hand and stroked her arm, feeling the goose bumps erupt beneath his touch.

'Don't do that, Louis.'

'What?' He eyed her innocently.

'Touch me.'

'Sorry.' He leaned back in his chair. 'I couldn't resist it.'

She let it go. It would be so easy to take offence, and make a scene, but that was the last thing she wanted.

'Is the queen here?' she asked.

He nodded. 'She's in the north wing... miles away.'

'Your sister?'

'No, she's out on a date.'

'I didn't know she was dating anyone. There's been nothing in the papers, or on social media about it.'

'She's more discreet than I am.'

She arched a brow and made a show of searching the room with her eyes. 'I'm surprised not to find any paparazzi lurking behind the curtains, or under the table.'

'That's one of the reasons I had you brought here. I didn't think you'd appreciate the attention that dining out would bring.'

'One of the reasons?'

Louis' fingers flexed around his water glass. He knew he had to play it cool. 'I wanted you to see where I hang out.'

'When you're not hanging out in night clubs?'

'Yes, I suppose.' *God, she was blunt.* 'I thought...'

'That I might hanker after hanging out here myself... permanently?' She smiled to show that she was joking – or, at least, half-joking.

'You can obviously read me like a book. I'm not sure if I like that.'

She shrugged and took another dainty sip of champagne. 'You're pretty transparent, Louis.'

'I didn't think that was one of my many peculiarities.' In fact, it wasn't. It was strange how she could read him so well, when others couldn't even scratch the surface.

'You have peculiarities?' She raised a brow. 'Why don't you tell me some of your redeeming qualities? Tell me some things about yourself that have never reached the media.'

'Why?' He was nonplussed. 'Wouldn't you rather get to know me more naturally?'

'There won't be time for that. Remember – after your mother's dinner - you promised to leave me alone.'

'Yes, I do recall agreeing to that, but...

'No, *buts*, Louis – you promised.'

He had, more's the pity. 'Okay.' He thought a moment. 'I love animals.'

'I knew that already.'

'Yes, but I have four horses that I rescued from the abattoir.'

'I didn't know that.' She was quite surprised. 'Why didn't I know that?'

'Because no one but my immediate family and close associates know about it.'

'What else?'

'Well, let me think... I'm a pretty generous guy. The drinks are always on me.'

'You can afford it... that sort of generosity isn't a redeeming quality in itself.'

'No?'

She shook her head and took a long swallow of her drink, almost draining the glass. 'No. If you were a normal working man, it would be.'

'Then, I guess that – by accident of birth – you'll deny me every redeeming bit of character I possess?'

'Maybe. Try another one on me.'

He took his time. It was nigh on impossible to come up with a single trait that she would accept as genuine altruism, or a quality that would worthy to pass muster. Finally, he said, 'I'm selfless.'

She laughed and choked on the last of her champagne.

'Why is that funny?' The question came out sounding cold.

'Sorry. I'm sorry.' She buried her face in her napkin. 'It's just that you seemed so serious saying that when it's so obviously not true.'

'Who says that it's not true?' He was genuinely hurt. 'You don't know me, Felicity... not really. Ten years ago, I may have been a selfish arse, but that's not to say that I'm selfish now.'

She sobered. 'Okay, then explain to me why *you* think that you're selfless.'

He *could* explain. He could tell her that he was giving up the possibility of living a normal life just so that his mother could die in peace. He could tell her that he had selflessly agreed to marry, just to give the monarchy one last chance of survival. He could explain that he got out of bed most mornings – hangover or no hangover – to do what good he could for the country and the commonwealth. But he knew that he wouldn't tell her any of that.

'Cat got your tongue?'

'Something like that.'

'I've upset you.' Her eyes widened. 'My God, Louis, I've really upset you.'

'I'm not upset,' he lied. 'I think we should drop the subject and eat.' He signalled one of the footmen forward. 'Bring the food,' he said almost fiercely. 'It's probably getting cold.'

It was a wonderful meal, but everything tasted like mud in Felicity's mouth. She'd soured their evening with her questions, and she was abjectly sorry to have upset him. It was true that she didn't really know him. The Louis of ten years previously wasn't the Louis of today. In some ways, he seemed a worse version of himself, and, in other ways, he seemed better. He'd made an effort to wine and dine her and – unsurprisingly – to woo her, and she'd spoiled everything by being her usual unforgiving, brash self.

She loved what he'd done with the horses. It showed that – deep down – he was a kind man. She'd never imagined him as kind. What else was there about him that he'd kept hidden from the world?

After dessert, and when the coffee had been served, he dismissed the servants. The evening had drawn to a quick close, and the subject of marriage hadn't come up once.

Surprisingly, it was Felicity who finally raised it.

'I think that there's something you're not telling me about why it's so urgent that you get married,' she said. 'And, why – out of the women you could easily have – you want me. I've heard the *because you're sensible* routine, but I don't buy it.'

She'd been reading him again. He was mightily uncomfortable with that. He hoped her powers didn't extend to actually being able to read his mind, because she'd be shocked to learn just how badly he *did* want her.

Or perhaps she wouldn't be shocked at all? Perhaps she had enough of an inkling to realise that he saw her as unfinished business? He hadn't given up on the possibility of seeing her naked, and he didn't mind admitting to himself that making love to her would be one of the main perks of marrying her.

'Perhaps there is more of a reason,' he returned. 'But it's not my place to reveal it.'

'Not even to me... the woman you're trying to persuade to marry you?'

He shook his head. 'No.'

'So, I would have to take you on blind faith?'

'It would be a leap... yes.'

'What about my other question... why me? And don't say it's because I'm *sensible*.'

'It *is* because you're sensible,' he said.

'Flattery will get you everywhere.'

He forced a smile. 'It isn't only that.'

'Oh?'

'You're pretty easy on the eye.'

'So are most of the women you date.'

'Touché.'

'So, what else?'

'I like you.'

'Don't you like any of those other women?'

'No.' The word was bald and emphatic.

It shut her up. She had nothing to go back at him with. She pressed her palms on the table and stood. 'I think I'd better leave,' she said. 'It's getting late.'

He expelled a lungful of air. The night had been a disaster. He couldn't allow her to leave without at least one more attempt to persuade her.

'Sit with me a moment longer, Felicity... please.'

She dropped back into her seat. She knew that she should leave. It was folly to give him that other moment, but – after literally eviscerating him with her observations - she felt that she owed him at least that much.

'Say it, then,' she prompted. 'Get it off your chest.'

He dragged in a breath, reached over, and took her hand, and said, 'Will you do me the honour of being my wife, Felicity?'

Chapter Eight

It was the day before her birthday dinner, and Louis could see that his mother was feeling the effects of unusual anxiety about the event. She had two birthdays every year – her real one, and her official one. The dinner was to celebrate the real one. Normally, only close family attend the private dinner. There was great celebration, including the Trooping of the Colour – for the official day, and opening her home to a large group of dignitaries on the date of her birth not only went against tradition, but ran the risk of offending a great many people. It was perfectly all right to be excluded from a quiet family affair, but quite another to be denied an invitation when others, so obviously less worthy, were being made welcome.

Her motivation was two-fold – to hopefully introduce her son's fiancé to the world, and to have one final, extravagant birthday celebration around her own dinner table before she died.

But, the planning, and the consequences of having such a small number of guests – one hundred was quite a small number considering how many actually wanted an invitation – was taking its toll on her patience and her temper.

As usual, she took it out on Louis.

'Who was that woman you were photographed with last night?' she asked, looking down her long nose at Louis and frowning.

'Woman?' Louis knew exactly who his mother meant, but he had no intention of owning up to anything. His private life – what little he had – was his own business.

'The one who was very nearly dressed, and who was hanging all over you outside that club in Soho.'

'Oh, *that* woman?' He grinned and shrugged. 'Just a friend of a friend.'

'Indeed? Well, she was certainly very friendly.'

Coming from anyone else, that statement would've sounded like humour, but, from his mother, it came across as acidic censure.

'Yes, she's a very friendly girl.'

'You have to stop all this nonsense, Louis. It's precisely that sort of behaviour that's bringing us all down.'

'Hardly,' he muttered under his breath.

'When you're married...'

'*If* I get married. Nothing is certain.' After their dinner date – which hadn't ended quite as disastrously as he thought - he was hopeful, but he didn't feel it appropriate to get his mother's expectations up just yet.

'Oh, it *is* certain. If not Felicity... then someone else. I won't be thwarted on this.'

He rolled his eyes. He wished she would drop the whole thing. It wasn't going to work, anyway. If the Prime Minister was bent on destroying them, then his marriage wouldn't necessarily stop it from happening.

He was willing to try – he owed his parents, and the country, that much – but he was becoming increasingly concerned about how many lives would be ruined in the process.

'I'm beginning to think that Felicity isn't the right one,' the queen said, matter of fact. 'I know she's my best friend's daughter, and has at least half of a good bloodline, but she's too opinionated. I'm concerned that she won't make you a good wife, and an even worse queen.'

'That's utter rubbish, mother.' He felt an urge to defend her. 'She's a modern woman, in a modern time. She'd make a perfect queen.'

'Really? I don't think I've seen you this animated for a long time. Don't tell me that you actually like her.'

'I like her well enough.' His expression darkened. 'Well enough not to hear her maligned.'

'She's *my* subject. I can malign her all I want.'

Louis groaned inwardly. That statement spoke volumes and was reflective of everything that was wrong with the monarchy. His dalliances with women, and his oft-times wild behaviour, had nothing – or certainly very little – to do with the popularity of the crown diminishing. It was his mother's arcane beliefs, and her strict adherence to out-dated protocols that were at the root of the PM's insistence that the country no longer wanted or needed them.

She'd become worse since the illness had become known to her. She no longer had patience or a flexibility in her thinking. She now tended to alienate, where once she'd charmed.

He felt heart-sorry for her. She was dying and the only thing that eased the thought of it was the hope that he'd marry and secure her throne. He had to be kind to her. He had to do everything in his power to make her end as comfortable as possible – no matter the cost to him.

'She's really very sweet,' he said, his voice soft. 'She's not malleable... I know that... but she's intelligent, and she's loyal. There's nothing wrong with having a little bit of spirit, mother. A queen needs spirit.'

'If only there was time,' she said. 'Your future bride will require a great deal of preparation. It's not an easy role to take on. I fear that Felicity would tug at the bit a little too much.'

He found himself agreeing with that observation. Felicity would never allow herself to be placed in harness. She'd insist on going her own way, and at her own pace. Look at how she'd refused to make love to him. No other woman had ever refused him. She'd stuck to her guns, regardless of the consequences, and now – in spite of their shared chemistry - she was still refusing him. She would never bow to pressure. She would never go against her own instincts. She would never blindly follow the rules required of the wife of the heir to the throne.

But rather that than a meek and obedient drone, he mused.

The queen knew exactly what her son was thinking. She knew that he was only agreeing with the whole marriage thing to please and ease her, but she also knew that it wouldn't take much to make him withdraw from the whole idea. Despite what she'd intimated, she actually wanted Felicity, and not simply because she was her friend's daughter. She would never put friendship above what her country needed and, if the girl had been anyone other than who she was, then nothing would have persuaded her to choose her.

She regretted many things in her life - most of all she lamented her indifference to what was happening around her. She'd been too proud, too autocratic, and too reliant on hundreds of years of history to pay heed to the discontent, and the whisperings of the republicans. It was time for a new generation to take the royal family forward, and to save what she'd almost destroyed.

She didn't want a clone of herself on the throne when she was gone. She didn't want her son married to anyone who would adhere to granting his every whim. She wanted someone strong and with character to sit on his right side.

She knew, full well, Louis' history with Felicity. There wasn't anything about her son that she didn't know. The girl had shown herself to have gumption. As much as she admired Felicity's mother, she couldn't help but be impressed that she'd raised such a level-headed, sensible child. It suggested to her that the girl's character, her intelligence, and her independence had benefitted from the mix of genes brought about through her mother's marriage to a commoner, because those traits certainly didn't come solely – if at all - from her mother.

She had to make Louis fight for her, and the only way she knew how to do that was to disparage her, and to suggest that another woman would be better suited to be his wife. Louis was a man who always hankered after what he thought he couldn't have. He was also kind enough to want to protect and stand up for someone he believed was being wrongly maligned. Add to the mix the horror of having his own mother choose his bride, and she was ensuring, by her words and actions, that he'd do his utmost to secure Felicity's acceptance of his proposal.

'There can be no more photographs,' she said. 'I hope you realise that?'

He sighed and nodded. She was right – of course, she was right. He would have to learn to be more discreet.

They were disturbed by a knock on the sitting-room door. It was Horace, the queen's personal secretary - a small man who was universally disliked amongst the royal household, and a person who Louis didn't trust an inch.

Most of what reached his mother's ears came from Horace. Every newspaper article, every social media post, every bit of gossip was gleefully passed on to her, and the oily little snake basked in the knowledge that he was causing pain all around.

Louis ignored his entrance. He made a point of never acknowledging him, and very rarely looked in his direction. He knew that Horace didn't mind that one little bit.

Louis wanted to leave them to it, but something held him in the room. He heard Felicity's name being mentioned, and his ears pricked up.

His mother threw him a furtive glance. Something was obviously up.

'What?' he said.

Horace turned beady little eyes on him, a smirk hovering below the surface of his lips.

'I felt I had to share a piece of news with her majesty,' he said.

'About Felicity?'

He gave a curt nod. 'It seems that she has a ... well, the only way I can describe it is to say – she has a lover.'

Louis knew that his mouth was hanging open, but he couldn't make his brain send the message to close it.

A lover? Felicity?

He shook his head.

'It's only a rumour,' the queen put in. 'I wouldn't jump to any conclusions.'

'Oh, it's perfectly true,' Horace insisted. 'I have it straight from the horse's mouth.'

'What horse would that be?' Louis asked, finally making his mouth work.

'The lover, of course.'

'Nonsense.' He couldn't bring himself to believe it. 'She would have told me.'

Horace raised an eyebrow. 'You think so, your highness? Why would she have done that?'

'As a reason not to marry me, of course.'

'If you say so, sir.'

Louis felt like punching him. He always felt like punching him, but never more so than at that moment.

He was lying. He had to be lying.

'Who is this man... this lover?' the queen asked.

'Robert Baker, ma'am. He's a solicitor at the firm where she works. I might add...' he cleared his throat and dropped is eyes. 'I might add that the man in question is currently married.'

'No!' Louis advanced towards him; his fists clenched at his sides. 'I don't believe you.'

But was it actually true? If it was then, of course, she would never have told him – not even to stop him pestering her.

A married man? It didn't bear thinking about.

'Why would he divulge that information to you?'

Horace looked directly at him. 'Because I heard rumours. Because I knew of the queen's... and your... plans. Because I wanted to ensure that she was properly vetted. I approached him, and point-blank asked him if the rumours were true.'

'And, he said that they were?'

'Indeed, yes. In the end, he was quite forthcoming.'

He was dumbfounded. She hadn't surrendered herself to him, but had taken a married man to her bed? He wondered if the two-timing rat had taken her virginity. No, that wouldn't be the case. He knew how old she was. Who heard of a twenty-eight-year-old virgin?

'Leave us, Horace. I want to talk to the prince alone.'

Louis watched him bow and leave the room but, before his mother could utter another word, he strode after him.

He had the man's name, but he wanted more detail than that.

Chapter Nine

Something was off at work. The office was usually buzzing, but that morning there was a heaviness in the air and an atmosphere that seemed strained. The firm comprised of six partners and Felicity worked directly for Robert Baker who specialised in probate. When she arrived, just before nine o'clock, she was surprised to find his office empty. She checked his electronic diary, just in case she'd missed a meeting, and saw the whole day had been blocked out.

She compressed her lips and frowned. He hadn't mentioned anything to her, and she wondered who had cancelled his appointments, because she certainly hadn't. She walked through to the room she shared with one of the other legal secretaries.

'Mary, do you know where Robert is today?'

It was a straight-forward question. There was no need for Mary to throw her a hostile look, but a hostile look was exactly what she was thrown.

'What's going on? Has something happened?'

'*You* tell *us*, Felicity.'

'How would I know?'

She suddenly looks sheepish. 'I'm sorry. I thought...'

'What, Mary? Why is everyone avoiding looking at me? Even Sharon on reception didn't chirp her usual *good morning* when I arrived.'

Mary wasn't up to offering an explanation. She dropped her head and busied herself sorting through a sheaf of papers on her desk.

'Mary? Hello... Mary? Don't ignore me...What's going on?'

Mary straightened her spine and lifted her head, so she was looking directly up at her. 'You really don't know?'

'No,' she replied, perplexed. 'Why would I?'

'Because, after you left yesterday, Robert's wife put in an appearance.'

'Carole?' Felicity frowned, confused. 'So?'

'She was angry.'

'Carole is *always* angry. What has her visit to do with everyone treating me like a pariah?'

'She found out.'

'Stop being so cryptic, Mary, and spit it out. What does she know?'

'About you. She knows about you.'

Felicity waited for more and, when it wasn't forthcoming, she threw her hands in the air, and groaned, 'I give up. Whatever this is, keep it to yourself – see if I care.'

She placed her bag on the floor under her desk, sat down, and immediately switched on her computer. Even with Robert being out of the office, she still had plenty of work to do. She knew that Mary was watching her through lowered lids, and she knew that her colleague's brain was turning with thoughts of whether, or not, to give her the full story. Felicity was quite prepared to wait her out. Office politics bored her, and she'd already given the current situation too much of her time.

The office they shared was small, but it had a large window, so was bright with morning sunlight. Felicity had to squint to see what was on her screen. She had over thirty unread emails, but the one from Robert immediately grabbed her attention.

She opened it. It had been sent the previous evening. It had a one-word message.

Sorry.

She reared back from the screen.

What the..?

'Mary, why would Robert send me an email saying sorry?'

'For telling Carole, perhaps?'

'Telling Carole what?'

'About... you know what.'

'Jeeze... if I have to come over there, I'll shake an explanation out of you.'

'This isn't easy, you know. I'm your friend, Felicity... or, at least I thought I was. You should've told me.'

Felicity decided to lapse back into silent mode. Everyone – Mary included – thought that she was guilty of something. She wasn't going to play the guessing game any longer. Let them think what they liked.

A heavy silence descended, and Felicity refused to allow it to make her feel uncomfortable.

'I don't think Robert is coming back,' Mary finally blurted out.

Felicity flicked her a look but remained silent. She knew better than to stall her by asking the obvious.

'He took the photograph of Carole from his desk.'

Now, *that* was a serious act. That particular photograph was sacrosanct.

'Everyone thinks that Carole made him resign,' Mary went on, keeping a close eye out for an appropriate reaction from Felicity. She was disappointed when all she received was a blank look.

'Aren't you surprised... shocked?'

Felicity shrugged. 'He wouldn't leave - not just like that. He loves his job far too much to resign. You've obviously got your wires crossed.'

'Then, I guess that everyone has their wires crossed.'

'Everyone? You mean, everyone in the building thinks that – somehow - I'm responsible for whatever's happened to Robert?'

'That sounds about right.'

'Look...' Felicity moved out from behind her desk. 'Why don't you start at the beginning? Perhaps I'll be able to work out what's going on.'

'Okay.' Her face tightened. 'But don't shoot the messenger.'

'Jeeze, Mary – I don't have a gun in my handbag.'

'I was speaking metaphorically,' she returned, insulted.

'I know that.' She perched on the edge of Mary's desk 'Sorry... go on.'

'Right... well, you'd gone to the Town hall on some business, or other, and Robert was in his office with a client, when Carole came barging through the door as if her clothes were on fire. I tried to stop her interrupting Robert, but she went straight in and, a few moments later, the client came scurrying out, and I heard raised voices.' She stopped to catch her breath, then said, 'She was peppering every word with your name. Even though the door was closed, I could hear her loud and clear. Robert was shouting that she was deranged and that whoever told her that you, and he...' She brought her eyes up. 'Well, he shouted that it was all rubbish.'

'Robert, and me?'

'I think that was the gist of what that meant.'

'Then, what happened?'

'It went quiet for a bit, and then they both left. Robert didn't look the road I was on. It was as if I wasn't even there. He told Sharon on reception to make sure all his appointments were cancelled for today. I don't know why he told her to do that. In your absence, he should've asked me to do it.'

'Never mind that... what makes you think that he's resigned?'

'Because...' She rolled her eyes. 'Stephanie took a call from Carole last night. Would you believe she rang her at home?'

Stephanie was the managing partner's PA. Felicity knew she wasn't adverse to being contacted at home out of hours.

'What did she say to her?'

'That Robert wouldn't be coming back and that, if she had any sense, she'd see that you were fired.'

Gobsmacked was not the word. Felicity was absolutely dumbfounded.

'Surely no one thinks that I was having an affair with him?' Even as she spoke the words, and even as she realised how ridiculous they sounded, she knew that the answer would be a resounding *yes*.

The room began to spin. She thought she might faint.

'No way, Mary. No one can possibly believe that.'

Mary shrugged and dropped her eyes. 'I think that's what Carole believed.'

'Well, Robert will disabuse her of that.'

She brought her eyes back up. 'He obviously didn't, or he'd be here, wouldn't he?'

'Yes, but – it's ridiculous.'

'She always was a bit touched in the head. She probably just got hold of the wrong end of the stick.'

It was obvious that Mary didn't believe her own words. Her expression belied every single one of them.

Felicity got to her feet. 'I'm going upstairs to have a word with Stephanie.'

'Is that a good idea?'

'Why wouldn't it be? I've not done anything wrong. I just want to ensure that she, and Mr. Johnson, are made aware of that fact.'

Without further ado, she marched from the office and up the single flight of stairs to the executive suite.

Stephanie was on the phone and, on seeing Felicity loitering in the open doorway, raised a finger and bid her wait.

It was a complicated, long drawn-out telephone call, and Felicity waited a full ten minutes before she was waved in.

'I wondered how long it would take you to show your face up here,' Stephanie said without any preamble. 'I suppose you've come to say that you know nothing about that debacle in Robert's office yesterday?'

'Only what Mary just told me,' she replied defensively.

'So, Robert didn't ring you to fill you in... warn you?'

'Why would he do that? His marriage problems have nothing to do with me.'

'Carole thinks otherwise.'

'Well, Carole is wrong, and that's what I've come up here to tell you. I'd appreciate a word with Mr. Johnson, and I'd be grateful if you would use the grapevine to squash this stupid rumour.'

'Mr Johnson is busy. As you can imagine, he has a great deal to sort out. Robert has a client list a mile long, and him leaving has dropped the firm right in it.'

'I know all the clients, perhaps I can...'

'No, Felicity. You can't do anything. 'Mr. Johnson doesn't want any help from you. And – as for me squashing the rumour – I'm afraid that's beyond my capabilities.'

Her eyes flared. 'Am I fired?'

'We're invoking the *no fraternisation* clause in your contract.'

She dragged in a steadying breath. 'There was no *fraternisation*. Why won't you believe me?'

'Simple... Robert confirmed the affair to Mr. Johnson.'

Chapter Ten

She craved a drink. Anything alcoholic would suffice. The fridge's only offering was the dregs of a bottle of week-old wine.

It wasn't enough, so she headed for her mother's private sitting room, where she knew there was a bottle of vodka in the drink's cabinet with her name on it. It might be an hour short of lunch time, but she didn't care. She was going to get drunk.

The raw vodka went down a treat and, after two glasses, she felt marginally better.

All the way back, from what she'd once known as her place of work, Felicity had fumed. She didn't know who she was most angry at – Robert Baker for his lies, or Stephanie and the managing partner for believing him. She didn't know what had possessed her boss to admit to such a blatant lie, but – whatever had driven him to own up to something so ridiculously untrue – she would get to the bottom of. She knew where he lived and, after she'd calmed down, she planned to confront him.

Instead, she decided that alcohol – as an immediate panacea – was preferable to a slanging match on Baker's doorstep.

She stumbled up the stairs and headed for her bedroom, the bottle of vodka held tightly against her chest. She was grateful that her mother didn't often emerge from her own room much before noon, so she didn't have to face her with an explanation as to why she was at home and not at work, and why she was half sozzled at eleven o'clock in the morning.

She loved her bedroom. It was her sanctuary. Painted in a pretty lilac, it was bright and cheery, and big enough for a king-sized bed, as well as a plush sofa, an antique dressing-table, and a wall of wardrobes.

It was at the back of the house, so it looked out over the small court-
yard-cum-patio and provided views across the fence to the metropolis
that was London.

She decided to phone Alice. Her friend would commiserate with
her predicament and give her some advice. On second thoughts, she decided that her father was a better bet. Alice was a good friend, but she
had a mouth that she found difficult to keep closed. Her supposed affair with a married man – although completely untrue – would quickly do the rounds of their mutual friends, and – no doubt – go beyond
their intimate circle, courtesy of Facebook and Twitter.

But it was barely six o'clock in the morning in New York – London
being five hours ahead – so, her father would still be in bed. It was a sad
state of affairs that – when she desperately needed someone to talk to,
to confide in - she had no one.

She could ring Louis.

No way.

How stupid an idea was that?

*Hey, Louis... guess what? Apparently I'm having an affair with my
married boss, and I've just been sacked over it. Fancy coming over to help
me commiserate over a bottle of vodka.*

Yeah, right.

She kicked off her shoes and crawled across the bed. Propped up
against the pillows, she took a long swallow straight from the bottle.
She'd needed that job, and she'd probably never get any references to
enable her to get another.

What had Baker been thinking? She'd never spoken to him outside
of the office, never mind have a fling with him. He was almost twenty
years her senior, and not in the least attractive – not that she would
have ever considered a relationship with him if he'd been younger, fit-
ter, and drop-dead gorgeous. Married men were way out of bounds.

She drew her mind back over the past couple of weeks. He hadn't
seemed to act strangely around her. He hadn't tried to make a pass at

her, be rebuked, and then decided to take revenge by making up an horrendous lie and getting her sacked. Everything had been perfectly normal. Nothing strange had happened between them. He had done his job, and she had done hers, and that had been the extent of it.

So, what had he been playing at, and why had he left the firm? He'd been there for over twenty years, was a partner, and seemingly loved what he did. Probate was boring, but he'd found his niche, and seemed happy enough.

Confused, she took another pull on the bottle.

She had to get her job back. They had no right sacking her. They were lawyers – they should've known better.

She'd sue their asses.

What with? You have no money.

That was true. Perhaps her father would lend her enough to cover her legal costs? He was always trying to give her money, but – apart from cash gifts on her birthday, and at Christmas – she'd always refused. She'd wanted to earn her own living.

But this was different. She wouldn't be able to earn a penny without references.

She looked at her watch. It was still far too early to ring him.

She blew out a long breath. She didn't deserve anything that was happening to her. She had a playboy prince stalking her and threatening to break her heart all over again. She had a best friend who she couldn't turn to because she couldn't keep a secret. She had a mother who wanted to sacrifice her future happiness in favour of her own, and she now had no job, and probably a reputation as a home-wrecker.

What was fair about any of that?

The acid burn of the vodka jolted her from the bed, and she was soon heaving over the rim of the toilet in her adjacent bathroom, emptying her stomach and wishing she was dead.

With a woozy head causing her to stagger, she made her way back to the bed. She'd had enough vodka. Getting drunk hadn't been such a good idea after all.

Alarmed by a knock on the door, she buried herself under the quilt and feigned sleep. She was sure it was her mother looking to find out why she was at home. She'd see her in the bed, and surmise that she'd come home sick from work.

The door creaked open. She didn't move.

'Felicity?'

It *was* her mother.

'What's wrong? Are you sick?'

Still, she didn't move.

'Is that a bottle of vodka?' Her voice was raised in shock.

Felicity heard her heavy tread as she crossed the floor towards her. A huge dose of trouble was about to descend on her head.

The quilt was dragged from around her, and she found herself peering up and into a very angry countenance.

Her mother was rather ugly when her face was contorted in fury.

She grabbed back the quilt and threw it over her head.

'I'm ill,' she groaned. 'Leave me alone.'

'I *will not* leave you alone. I want an explanation.'

'I don't have one.'

'Felicity! Sit up!' She yanked on the quilt once more. 'I want to know what's happened. It smells like a brewery in here.'

'Vodka doesn't smell,' she returned, finally releasing the quilt, and pulling herself up onto her elbows. 'I got sacked from work,' she said. 'Happy, now?'

She expected an angry retort, but her mother simply stared down at her in silence.

'Did you hear what I just said? I've been sacked. I am no longer gainfully employed.'

'I heard you. I'm just wondering what to say in answer to that little piece of news.'

'I didn't do anything wrong.' There were tears in her voice. 'They said... they said that I broke the terms of my contract... I didn't.'

'What terms?'

'Does it matter?'

'Of course, it matters. It could have ramifications.'

'Ramifications?' She screwed up her eyes. 'Oh, you mean that, if I did something really bad, it would spoil your plans for me and Louis?' She suddenly felt like smirking. If her mother only knew...

'Tell me,' she said. 'I have the right to know.'

'Later.' She flopped onto her back and brought the quilt up and under her chin. 'After I've had a nap, and after I've had a chance to speak to dad.'

'You should tell me, before you speak to *him*. You live under my roof, Felicity. I'm the one you should consider first.'

'Oh, mum... I wish you'd leave me alone. Sometimes you're just a bit too much to deal with.'

'Really? I didn't think I'd raised you to be so ungrateful.'

'I'm not ungrateful. I appreciate the roof you've continued to put over my head, but it doesn't give you the right to try and rule me.'

They stared at one another. Her mother dropped her eyes first.

'Very well,' she said, turning back towards the door. 'You know where I'll be when you're ready to talk.'

The silent scream bouncing inside her brain made her head throb – either that, or the vodka. She thought there might be a paracetamol or two in her bag, but it was way over the other side of the room, and she didn't have the energy to fetch it.

She lay there and suffered the headache, until the remnants of the alcohol rushing through her bloodstream rendered her unconscious.

Chapter Eleven

S he was surprised not to hear a peep from Louis. The queen's dinner party was a mere few hours away, and he hadn't texted or rang her. Normally, she would be relieved not to be bothered by him, but his silence so close to their *date* was disarming.

She itched to contact him, hoping he'd changed his mind about her invitation. She really wasn't in the mood to smile and chat with strangers, and she certainly wasn't in the mood for any more of the POW's cack-handed attempts to sweep her off her feet.

She'd managed to speak to her father, but – where she'd expected some words of wisdom, and an offer to finance a court case, instead, she'd received a bland response that literally told her to forget it and move on. *Move on where*? she'd asked, perplexed at his apparent laissez-faire attitude. His response to her question wasn't helpful, and he'd ended the conversation with a promise to ring her back another time to discuss it.

Surprisingly, her mother seemed a little more sympathetic, but she, too, erred on the side of *leave it alone*. Of course, her motive was entirely selfish. She didn't want the queen, or Louis, getting wind of it. *There can be no hint of scandal*, she'd said. *Keep quiet, and it will blow over.*

Neither parent seemed in the least interested that she'd lost her job, or in the fact that it would be impossible to find another, equally suitable, one.

Her mother had simply looked at her with a knowing smile on her face, which Felicity clearly read as meaning she wouldn't need a job - not when she was married to the Prince of Wales.

If she hadn't known any better, she would've believed that her mother had orchestrated the whole thing.

Flushed from the shower, she stood in front of the wardrobe and eyed the dress her mother had bought especially for the dinner party. It was three-quarter length, pale blue, and rather too flowy for her taste. It had cost an absolute fortune. Until it was fully paid for, she imagined they'd be living on baked beans.

The only thing that the dress had going for it was that it complemented her eyes. She certainly didn't think it would do anything to accentuate her figure.

She really ought to have tried it on in the boutique, but she hadn't been in the least interested in twirling in front of a mirror for her mother's benefit.

It slid from the hanger and seemed like a rag in her hands. Considering how much it cost, it was hardly substantial. As she slipped it over her head, she half-hoped that it wouldn't fit.

Her eyes nearly popped out of her head when she caught sight of her reflection.

Demure, Felicity – that's what's called for, her mother had said when she'd chosen the dress off the rack. *A future queen shouldn't flash her body-bits to all and sundry.*

Well, her mother would certainly get a shock when she got an eyeful of her daughter's breasts pouring out over the rather low-cut bodice.

Actually – when, half an hour later, she presented herself - her mother looked at her with a smug expression on her face.

'He won't be able to take his eyes off you,' she said. 'I'll be surprised if you don't come home with a ring on your finger tonight.'

Felicity groaned and nudged her breasts self-consciously. She was a jeans and sweater kind of girl. She preferred dressing down, as opposed to wearing any fancy frippery. And, as for make-up? She thought she looked like a clown.

'What about jewellery?' Her mother arched a brow. 'You look very bare around the neck.'

'I don't have anything suitable,' she returned.

'Well, I have just the thing.'

She marched from the room and was gone for long minutes. When she returned, she handed Felicity a fine gold chain with a beautiful, mounted pearl hanging as a pendant.

'That's...'

'Yes – an anniversary gift from your father.'

'It's very beautiful.'

'Hmmm.' Her mother sniffed and fastened the clasp behind Felicity's neck. 'I never much cared for it,' she said. 'It's rather too plain for me, but it suits you.'

The pearl sat snugly between her breasts. She knew it would draw the eye. She didn't think that wearing it was such a good idea. She reached back to unclip it, but her mother slapped at her hands.

'Leave it on,' she said sharply. 'It never brought me much luck, but perhaps it'll do better for you.'

'You're going to be awfully disappointed,' she said. 'I'm attending this dinner on sufferance, and not as a preamble to an engagement.'

'We'll see.'

'Yes, mum... we'll see.'

'Try and put a smile on your face,' she snapped. 'You're not heading off to your execution.'

'That's what it feels like,' she mumbled in return.

'Nonsense. You'll have a wonderful time. Goodness, Felicity, I wish you'd realise just how fortunate you are.'

'And I wish that you'd stop trying to push me down a path that I know will be treacherous.' She threw herself down onto the sofa. 'I've a good mind not to go.'

'I've made my feelings perfectly clear. If you carry on acting like this, I'll never speak to you again. Do you want that, Felicity? Do you want to turn me against you?'

'When have you ever been *for* me, mum? She felt the first sting of tears. She was about to ruin her mascara. 'This is all about you... not me.'

'You can see it that way, if you want, but – mark my words – if you refuse him again, I'll never forgive you. Now, get up, and go and wait on the car arriving.'

She stood. 'Tell me, again why you're not coming with me? It's not like you to give up the chance to dine at the palace. Is it because you think you might weaken and come to my rescue?'

The words were meant sarcastically. Her mother's motives for declining the queen's invitation weren't in the least altruistic. She hadn't explained her change of mind, and Felicity couldn't help but be suspicious.

'Well?' she prompted. 'Why did you change your mind?'

'I won't run the risk of being humiliated in front of everyone. I have no idea of how you will behave tonight, and I'd rather not witness you showing yourself... and me... up.'

'Do you have *no* faith in me?' she asked, hurt all over again at her mother's poor judgment of her. 'I can turn him down without making a scene.'

'That remains to be seen.'

'Well, you certainly won't be there to see it. I would've appreciated knowing you were there, and in my corner.'

'I *am* in your corner – if only you'd realise that.'

'How can you be? If you're dead set against me living my own life, and making my own decisions, how can you even say that?'

'Because it's true.

'Well, you go right on ahead believing that mum, but I never will.'

'Make your choice, and be done with it,' she ground out. 'But remember the consequences of denying him. Do you realise that, if you reject Louis, the queen will refuse to be my friend? Do you understand what that would mean for me?'

'I can't be responsible for the break-up of a fickle friendship.' Her voice sounded much stronger than she felt. 'You can't barter my happiness for your own.'

'So, refuse him. I'm sick of arguing the point with you.' She turned her back. 'Just don't come back here if you do.'

'You don't mean that?'

'Oh, but I *do* mean it.' She threw herself back around to face her daughter. 'How will you manage without a job? How will you afford a place of your own with no money coming in?'

She swallowed back hard. 'My father...'

Her mother let out a brittle laugh. 'Your father has other fish to fry. Do you know that he's seeing someone?' She smiled a toothy grin. 'He's already distancing himself from you, isn't he?'

She didn't believe it. Her father would have told her if he'd met someone.

'Believe it, Felicity. You're father has finally moved on, and I don't think his new partner will be enthusiastic about a hanger-on as a step-daughter. Now, if you were engaged to Louis...' She left the remaining words unsaid. Her point had been well made.

She felt like a weak-minded little girl. All her life, she'd went along with whatever her mother had wanted. At her age, she shouldn't be living at home, and she certainly shouldn't be allowing herself to be dictated to. If her father had, at last, found happiness with another woman – well, good for him. She knew that she ought not to be dependent on him, any more than she was on her mother.

The truth of her life shocked her. Everything she was, and everything she'd ever done, was all down to her – not her mother, not her father, and she certainly wasn't the person she was today because of Louis breaking her teenaged heart.

No, she had no one to blame but herself.

Well, she realised that it was time to stand up and be counted. She was going to dictate her own future, regardless of the consequences, and she was going to start with Louis.

Chapter Twelve

He saw her arrive. She looked stunning. He turned his eyes from the sight of her and engaged himself in conversation with the pretty daughter of the American Ambassador.

He couldn't understand why he was so angry. It wasn't as if her love-life was any of his business. But it stung – the revelation that she was having an affair with a married man. He'd thought her better than that. He'd held her up as someone worthy of his hand in marriage. He'd even considered being faithful to her - for a while anyway. And all the time that he was virtually prostrating himself at her feet, she was up to no good with her middle-aged boss.

If it wasn't all so tragic, he'd die laughing.

Stop thinking about her, he told himself furiously. *She's history.*

The queen had been incandescent with rage. If Felicity's mother hadn't cancelled at the last minute, he honestly believed that his mother would have verbally eviscerated her. She'd been all set to send a message, revoking Felicity's own invitation to the dinner, but he'd stayed her hand.

Let her come, he'd said to her. *Let me deal with her.*

He wondered how he was going to do *that*. How could he deal with her when he couldn't even bear the thought of speaking to her?

'Your highness?'

He dropped his eyes. The pretty young daughter of the American Ambassador was staring up at him, her rose-bud mouth open and her face all bright with expectation.

'Amber... sorry... I was miles away,' he said, taking her arm and steering her towards where he knew her seat to be at one of the long tables stretching the length of the room. 'Why don't you sit down, and I'll fetch you a drink?'

She nodded, pleased by his attention. She couldn't wait to facetime her friends later and tell them all about the gallant prince who'd swept her off her feet.

Louis left her and signalled to one of the footmen carrying a tray of champagne. He had no intention of taking the drink directly to her and instructed the footman to do just that.

Dinner wouldn't be served until after the queen made an appearance. Meantime, the guests were meant to mingle, make small-talk, and await her arrival.

He wasn't in the mood for small-talk and headed towards the doors that opened onto a small balcony. The balcony was a new addition to the outside wall of the ballroom. It made an excellent bolthole for those weary of the atmosphere. He would hide-out there until everyone was seated.

The cool night air soothed him and dampened down his anger. He silently berated himself for feeling so strongly about something that he had no control over, and something that he had no right judging.

But he'd chosen her. He'd put aside all thoughts of marrying anyone else because he'd thought her quite perfect. He didn't love her, but he'd wanted her. He'd thought that she would make a good wife, and that life would never be boring with her by his side. He'd even begun to feel bad about the way he'd treated her all those years ago – believing his behaviour back then was the reason for her refusing him now.

He felt such a fool. The innocent, virginal Felicity was nothing more than a fraud.

He swallowed hard and fisted his hands. The more he thought about it, the angrier he became. It was almost as if she'd set out to dupe him. All she'd had to do was explain that she wasn't free to marry him, and there would've been no hard feelings, and he wouldn't have been left feeling like a chump. He would've understood. She was a grown woman, and she was entitled to any grown-up relationship she chose.

He stood for long moments, looking out towards Westminster, and contemplating his next move. His mother remained insistent that he marry. She'd already put forward two names for his consideration. Her choices filled him with horror. Now that Felicity was well and truly out of the picture, he had to find someone else, or run the risk of his mother foisting one of her favourites on him.

Then there was the fact that he still had to work out what he was going to say to Felicity. He wished he'd taken his mother's advice and rescinded tonight's invitation, but he'd been determined to see her when she was out of her element, and caught off-guard, so he could give her a piece of his mind.

She'll name you a hypocrite and laugh in your face.

Would he blame her?

Yes.

At least he'd been honest with her. At least she knew what he was. Apart from his mother's illness, he'd been straight with her.

He was just beginning to calm his thoughts when he heard the door open behind him.

'Louis?'

He jerked back and swung round.

He didn't say her name. He simply stared at her.

'I saw you coming out here, and I wanted a word, so I followed you.'

He remained silent, and he saw her expression change as she became aware of the anger in that silence.

'I wondered why you didn't say hello when you saw me arrive.'

There were many things he could say in response to that. He could say that he knew all about her. He could say that she'd made a fool out of him, and that he'd never forgive her. He could call her names or spit some other poison at her. Instead, all he said was, 'Just go back inside,

Felicity. I don't want to talk to you,' before turning his back on her once more.

He realised that she hadn't moved. He felt her eyes on him. 'Didn't you understand what I said?' He kept his back to her. 'I don't want you here.'

'But you invited me. You sent me a card. Why would you do that if all you intended to do was to ignore me?'

He sighed. 'That was before.'

'Before what?'

'Just, *before*.'

'Okay.'

'Okay?' He swivelled around. 'Is that all you have to say?'

'I didn't think you wanted me to say anything.'

'I didn't... I don't.'

'Then, it doesn't matter, does it?'

She infuriated him. She had no right to stand there acting all put-out and indignant. He was the one who should be indignant.

'You really fooled me,' he said. 'I thought...' He didn't finish the sentence. She had a look of hurt innocence about her, and he reminded himself that who she slept with wasn't any of his business. She hadn't encouraged him in any way. In fact, she'd went out of her way to discourage him. He now knew why, but what he didn't know was why it made him so angry. He couldn't possibly expect her to still be a virgin, and it had been entirely up to her who she lost it to. He hated that it hadn't been him, but he couldn't hate her for choosing someone else.

He raked a hand through his hair. He had no clue how to handle the situation. Mouthing off at her wasn't exactly smart.

'I'm sorry,' he said. 'I realise my stupid pursuit of you was terribly annoying. Your boyfriend...'

'My boyfriend?'

He was almost taken in by her look of confusion, and then he remembered that her affair with the solicitor was supposed to be a secret.

'I know... okay? I know all about your... *boyfriend*.'

She screwed up her face. 'I don't have a boyfriend.'

He gave her a knowing smile. 'If you say so.'

'No, honestly...'

'*Honestly*? You think having it off with a married man is honest?'

'What?' She stepped back in shock. 'You think...?'

'I don't *think*, Felicity... I *know*.' He took a step towards her, maintaining their distance. 'You should have told me, and I would've stopped chasing after you like an idiot.' He sighed, annoyed with himself more than her. 'I've wasted so much time on you. You must've had a good laugh over that.'

She took another step back. 'This is ridiculous, you're jumping to conclusions. You're making assumptions about me, based on what?'

'Based on what your lover told me.'

'What my *married* lover told you?' It was almost funny. She almost laughed. 'And who is he? Does he have a name?'

'Robert. His name is Robert, but you already know that.'

'The only Robert I know is Robert Baker.' Realisation dawned. The rumour had obviously spread to his ears. 'You think I'm having an affair with Robert Baker?'

He merely glared at her, his eyes smouldering with distaste.

She held up a hand. 'I've heard enough. I won't stand here to be insulted by you, of all people.'

'Oh, you're good, Felicity. You're really good, but your innocent act doesn't fool me.'

Her expression took on a stunned look. She opened her mouth, then closed it again. She was in a world of emotional pain and confusion. Her heart beat painfully against her ribs, and time seemed to stand still. She found that she couldn't bear him thinking so badly of her. Despite everything, she never wanted to look sullied in his eyes.

She found her voice once more. 'You said that he told you... that Robert told you?'

'Yes.'

'How? When?'

'Does it matter?'

'Of course, it matters.' Her face was flushed, and her eyes sparked with suppressed rage. She spoke slowly, with great care, saying, 'There was a rumour at work. That rumour just got me fired. I'm wondering... did you have something to do with that?'

A gong sounded in the ballroom. Everyone was being summoned to their seats.

'Absolutely not,' he said. 'I don't know anything about you being fired.'

'I don't believe you. It would be just like you to do something like that.'

He was mortally offended. How could she think such a thing? He backed off and slumped against the railing. As far as he was concerned, the conversation was over.

She wasn't prepared to let it drop. 'You said that you spoke to my boss.'

He gave a curt nod.

'Why? What drove you to do that?'

He shrugged and turned his head to the side. He could no longer bear the sight of her.

Her voice thickened. She hitched in a breath. 'Tell me, Louis. I deserve that much, at least.'

Without turning back to look at her, he sighed, and said, 'I wanted to confirm what I'd heard.'

'What had you heard?'

'You know. It's obvious.'

'Not to me, it isn't.'

Fleetingly, it occurred to him that he was wrong. Her reaction wasn't what he'd expected, and he suddenly felt uncomfortable.

He hesitated. She looked shocked, angry, but certainly not guilty.

He said, 'Someone – who knew of my interest in you – thought it prudent to share some information with me. I won't say who... the identification of that person isn't relevant. I felt that I needed to confirm what I'd been told.' He finally turned his eyes back on her. 'I didn't want to believe it.'

'But you believed it enough to go and speak to Robert?'

He nodded. 'Yes, I spoke to him. I went to see him.'

She gave a bitter snort of laughter. 'This just gets better and better.'

He stopped breathing. He had an awful feeling that he was completely in the wrong. She looked so... so righteously offended.

'I want to hear all of it.'

'There's nothing much to tell.'

'All of it, Louis.'

He'd went directly from Horace and straight to see Baker. He tried to remember exactly what the man had told him.

He'd went to his home and arrived right in the middle of a fight between Baker and his wife. It had been a moment of madness – arriving unannounced at a total stranger's home - but he'd been determined to confirm the truth.

He'd been surprised by the look of the man. He was nothing special – older than Felicity by about ten or fifteen years, much too thin, and he had the arrogant posture of a man well used to getting his own way. He'd wondered how, a man such as him, had managed to seduce a woman like Felicity. What had been his secret?

Looking back, he recalled that it had been Baker's wife who'd told him, and not actually Baker himself. He'd just sat there, with his head in the air, and a haughty expression on his face, as his wife took great pleasure in maligning Felicity with hateful words of censure.

He jerked back to the present. 'What do you see in him? I mean... he's virtually an old man.'

She ignored his question. It was hardly relevant. 'You went to see him?' she prompted.

'At his house, yes.'

'And he openly admitted to having an affair with me?'

'No... it was his wife who filled in the details.'

'What details? How could there be details of something that *never* happened?'

'She was pretty explicit.' His mouth dropped into a sardonic sneer. 'She revelled in the telling.'

She closed her eyes against his accusatory and disgusted expression. *He really thought... he really believed...*

She was so mad, she could spit nails. He didn't know her at all. He'd wanted to marry her, and he didn't have an inkling of the sort of person she was. He believed that she was nothing more than a slut.

It was ironic really. If anyone was the slut, it was the Prince of Wales. He was a notorious womaniser, and – to cap it all off – he wasn't adverse to the odd dalliance with a married woman.

The hypocrite... the damned pretentious...

She felt her whole body deflate. *What defence could she make? Should she even try? What would be the point?*

'I see I've rendered you speechless. How apt.'

She closed her eyes and imagined herself flying at him and raking the skin off his face. His protection detail would probably shoot her, but it would be worth it to leave him scarred for life.

She opened her eyes and stared him straight in the face. It was a beautiful face made suddenly ugly.

'I don't ever want to hear you apologise to me,' she said. 'When you realise what an idiot you've been – *and you will realise it* – I want you to swallow down on any apology you will feel the need to make. I won't want to hear it.' She huffed in a breath. 'It will be too late for regret.'

'There will be no fear of that.'

Solemnly, she shook her head. 'Famous last words.' She turned to leave, stopped, and said, 'I don't want to see you again... ever. Please don't try to contact or visit me.'

She walked away.

Stunned, he stood and silently watched her go. He watched through the glass in the doors as she made her way across the ballroom, past the rapidly filling tables, and out to the main foyer, where she disappeared from view.

He felt completely wrong-footed. He had no idea what had just happened. She was in the wrong, so why did he feel like such a heel?

He did know one thing – he would never apologise to her. Hell would freeze over first.

Chapter Thirteen

H ow was she supposed to get home? She didn't think she could
very well call a taxi and ask to be picked up at Buckingham
palace. They'd think it was a crank call. She wondered if she could simply walk out without being stopped. Was it common for people who'd
been invited to dine with the queen to simply walk out and catch a bus
home? She thought not.

She wouldn't go home. She wouldn't be welcome. She would have
to impose on Alice.

She stood at the top of the staircase, her legs barely holding her upright, and searched in her small clutch-bag for her phone.

No signal.

She almost snorted out a laugh. How could Buckingham palace
not have a phone signal? It was surreal.

'Can I help you, miss?'

Her head snapped back. Towering over her was a man clearly confused by her presence outside the ballroom.

'Are you lost?'

She shook her head and tucked her phone back into the bag. 'No,
I'm leaving,' she said, then inanely added, 'My phone doesn't have a signal.'

'No, it wouldn't... not here,' he said, smiling with his eyes. 'You're
not staying for dinner?'

'No, I'm...'

'Yes,' a voice said from behind her. 'She *is* staying for dinner. I'll es-
cort her back to the ballroom.'

She felt a hand on her arm. It burned her skin. It took every ounce
of self-control not to turn around.

'Very well, your highness,' the man said with a curt nod.

Felicity watched as he made his way down the wide staircase. If he'd been affected by Louis' appearance, and his insistence that she wasn't leaving, he didn't show it.

'I'm not done with you,' Louis said from behind her. 'And it's the height of bad manners to walk out on the queen.'

His breath caressed her neck. She shivered.

He pulled on her arm. 'Come back with me. We'll finish our conversation after dinner.'

'No,' she said, yanking her arm free and rounding on him. 'We've got nothing left to talk about, and I'm sure the queen will be relieved that I've left.'

'Maybe, but, I insist.' He took hold of her hand and pulled her back in the direction of the ballroom. 'Stop being such a child, Felicity, and behave.'

'*Behave?*' she spluttered. 'Are you for real?'

He shook his head, impatience sparking his eyes. 'She's just about to arrive. You have to be in your seat before she gets there... it's protocol.'

'Stuff protocol... I'm not going.'

'Oh, but you *are*.' He hauled her forward, almost dragging her off her feet. 'Your absence will be noted, and there will be questions. An empty seat at the table will stand out.'

'Too bad.' She dug in her heels and tried desperately to stop her forward momentum, but he was much too strong.

At the door, she had no choice but to stop her struggles and enter the room. Despite her desire to flee, she refused to make a scene. If she did, her mother would not only disown her, but probably have a stroke when she heard about it.

With seconds to spare, she took her seat. All eyes were turned on her as Louis deposited her, before making his way to the top table where he would sit on the queen's right.

Magnificent golden centrepieces filled with fresh flowers, ran the whole length of the table. An array of highly polished cutlery, pyramids of erect linen napkins, and exquisite crystal glasses dressed the remainder of the table and, such were their brilliance, that Felicity had to blink to focus her attention.

She didn't want to be there, but she couldn't help but feel a tiny bit privileged.

Two hours had never dragged so much in her life. She hardly tasted the food. Her stomach churned the whole time. When it was over, and the speeches began, she wished she could slip away unnoticed.

She wasn't sure what remained for Louis to talk about. If he wanted to berate her even further, he was going to be out of luck. She couldn't imagine him manhandling her in front of everyone to haul her, struggling, to a quiet corner. She had no intention of subjecting herself to any more of his sneering censure, and she wouldn't go quietly.

The unexpected happened. Louis didn't approach her alone. He brought the queen.

People parted before her, like the wash breaking from an ocean liner. She looked neither to the right, nor to the left, and made no acknowledgement of the bows and curtseys that saluted her. As she approached, her eyes never left Felicity's face.

It was suddenly so very warm. Felicity felt faint. Her knees buckled into a deep curtsey, and she wobbled precariously as she rose.

The queen had singled her out. It was the worst thing possible, and she wished she could melt into the floor.

'Good evening, Felicity,' she said in her familiar, cultured voice. 'How are you?'

'I'm well, your majesty, thank you.' She daren't look at Louis. She kept her eyes downcast. 'I want to thank you for the invitation.'

With a flick of a finger, the queen sent the nearby onlookers away.

'I feel the invitation was an error of judgement.' She said, glancing at her son. 'I was informed that you attempted to rectify that by leaving before dinner?'

Felicity swallowed anxiously. She sensed the underlying rancour in the queen's tone. Louis had obviously told her about the Robert lie.

Felicity had met the queen on several occasions, but mostly when she'd been a child, and her mother had brought her along to take tea with her. She remembered her as a formidable woman – most unlike her portrayal on television – and she'd grown up very much in awe of her. To be on the receiving end of her displeasure was, to say the least, disconcerting.

He should have let her leave. Oh, how she wished he'd allowed her to escape.

'Louis... the Prince of Wales... asked me to stay,' she replied - lying to keep the peace.

'Yes, he said as much.'

Louis cleared his throat and had the grace to drop his eyes.

'I'm in rather a quandary,' the queen said.

Felicity raised her head. 'Your majesty?'

'A quandary, Felicity... a troublesome quandary.' She narrowed her eyes. 'No matter... I'm sure you'll help me to overcome it.'

'Of course,... if I can.'

'We will speak on it later.' And, on those words, she swept away.

Louis hovered at Felicity's elbow. 'She insisted,' he said. 'I couldn't stop her.'

'What does she want from me?' she hissed up at him.

He shrugged. 'I have no idea.'

They were both aware of people staring. Some of the guests knew Felicity. Some were good friends of her mother. Others, although complete strangers, seemed to have a rapt desire to rake their eyes the length and breadth of her. They were all curious as to why she had received the queen's personal attention, and they were equally curious as to why the Prince of Wales looked so intense standing at her side.

'I hoped that – now dinner is over – I could leave,' she said.

'Not a good idea. She wants to speak to you. It's best to stay until she's done with you.'

'She can't make me, can she?'

'Don't be ridiculous,' he snapped. 'You're not a prisoner, or a hostage.'

'Well, you could've fooled me. *You* forced me to stay for dinner.'

'That was different and keep your voice down... you're drawing attention.'

Indignation straightened her spine. She looked directly up at him, wanting to say something really clever and really hurtful – something that would make him clamp his mouth tight shut – but no words came to mind.

She was well and truly freaked-out. So much had been said already, and now the queen had something to add to the mix. She dreaded what it might be.

'Look,' he said, taking her arm. 'Why don't you go and powder your nose... freshen up... take a moment to yourself? This is one giant fishbowl, and you're beginning to come apart at the seams.'

'Not until you give me some idea of what's going on,' she said. 'You need to give me an inkling of what your mother wants with me.' She cocked her head to the side. 'Does she know about Robert?'

'The Robert who *isn't* your boyfriend?'

'Yes, *that* Robert,' she returned snappily.

'She found out about him the same time as I did.'

Her eyes were wide and shocked. Her face was numb. She couldn't believe what he'd just said, and she had to work really hard to maintain her composure.

'What did you just say?'

'I said...'

'No.' She flapped a hand at him. 'Don't repeat it. I heard it the first time.'

'I don't think that's what she wants to talk to you about, so there's no need to get all agitated.'

'She said that she's in a quandary. Do you know what she meant?'

'I might.'

'Care to share?'

'It's not for me to say.'

'So, you're not going to say anything? You're going to stand back and watch me enter the lion's den without any idea of what she might say to me?'

'You're a big girl... you can take care of yourself.'

'I could just walk right out of here,' she said. 'After all, I'm not a prisoner.'

'Or a hostage.' The merest hint of a smile touched his lips. 'Why don't you try?'

'Leaving?'

He nodded.

She licked her lips and cast her eyes around her. If she tried to leave, would one of them jump on her, drag her back into the room?

Regardless, she knew that she couldn't stay. She looked at him a moment longer, then tore her eyes away. She mentally shook herself. The completely crazy moments that had peppered her life for weeks, had now culminated in being fired from work, being accused by Louis in a way that suggested she'd somehow been unfaithful to him, and finally being summoned to an audience with the queen.

She stood outside herself for a moment and dragged her mind over everything that Louis had said to her from the moment of his first proposal, to a few seconds ago.

She realised that she was being manipulated. All that nonsense about Robert was nothing more than a means to an end. Louis had been attempting to put her on the back foot, and it seemed that his mother was now primed to deliver the words that she hoped would ensure her surrender.

She wished she knew why. Nothing made sense. Her stomach turned to lead. They wanted to use her. She wasn't quite sure what that meant, but the truth of it was heart stopping.

Something was terribly amiss – something so profound that only marriage to her would put right. Ultimately, it wouldn't matter – her so-called affair with Robert. In fact, the lie might actually make them believe that she was ripe for the picking.

In this day and age? It can't be. It just can't.

The denial struck her as almost funny. Who was to say what could and couldn't be? People were always being used. Some were almost eaten alive by the selfish and the greedy.

The cruel thing was – the pitiful thing was – she was sorely tempted to allow herself to be eaten up.

She loved him.

'Please give my apologies to your mother,' she said. 'I'm afraid I can't stay.' The words almost choked her. They were the wrong words. In her mind, she was saying *yes* to everything. In her heart, she was wholly accepting, but her mouth would not permit her to betray herself. It defied her mind and her heart, and it saved her from herself.

'If you stay, you'll understand,' he said.

'I know,' she replied. 'But I don't want to understand.'

He frowned. 'I thought that, more than anything, that was what you truly wanted?'

'Perhaps, but it wouldn't be good for me. Knowing - understanding what's behind all this madness – would make me do something I knew to be wrong.'

'It wouldn't be wrong, Felicity.'

'Not for you.'

'Have I to give up on you?'

She gave that a moment's thought. 'Why hasn't your belief about Robert and me caused you to give up?'

He swallowed. 'That's in the past. I can put it to one side.'

'How very noble of you.'

'No, Felicity – not *noble*.'

'What, then?'

'Prudent.'

'Ah...' She gave a wan smile. 'I think I understand.'

'Please,' he said.

She walked away without another word.

Chapter Fourteen

She went home. She decided not to hide away at Alice's. She wanted to give her mother one more chance to step up as a parent, and back her decision. If she didn't, she would leave and never look back.

She listened outside the door to her mother's sitting room. Her hand hovered, ready to knock. A confrontation was inevitable, and - although she was keen to get it over with – something gave her pause. She'd just burned all her bridges with Louis, and she was hesitant of burning the final one with her mother.

It could wait until morning. There was no point in ending the night with even more high drama.

As she ascended the stairs to her bedroom, her tread was heavy. Knowing that she'd done the right thing hadn't lifted the weight from her mind. It hadn't eased anything.

Her head dizzy with thoughts and a multitude of regrets, she weaved across the floor, kicking off her shoes and pulling the dress from her body, and threw herself on top of the bed.

The silence in the room was deafening. She was alone, in the heavy quiet with nothing but her thoughts for company – and they made lousy company.

What had she done? It was all over now. There would be no more hot pursuit by Louis. She'd dissed his mother, walked away from him, and effectively ended any possibility of them ever being together.

Was that so terrible?

Yes!

Some things were becoming clear to her. She hadn't been as emphatically opposed to marrying him as she'd made herself believe.

She wished that she was eighteen again. No matter what had ultimately happened between them, she'd felt love from Louis for a time. Now, she wondered if she'd been deluding herself.

That summer had been so very special. The sun had never seemed to stop shining, the scent of apple-blossom always seemed to be in the air, and life had been glorious. In the ten years since, she couldn't recall ever feeling warm.

Louis had never been someone she'd admired from afar. They hadn't exactly grown up together, but she'd often been in his company, and – as a young boy – he was sensitive and attentive whenever her mother visited the queen and took her along.

In their early teenage years, she didn't see much of him and, what she did see, made her want to be more than an occasional acquaintance. It wasn't until she was eighteen, and he twenty, that they began dating.

By that time, he'd changed. Looking back, she knew that she should've noticed the difference in him, but – at the time – she was just grateful to be chosen as his girlfriend.

How pathetic, she silently railed at herself. *How absolutely pitiful.*

She scrubbed at her leaky eyes with the back of her hands and sniffed back the tears that threatened to overwhelm her. She wished that she could cease loving him. She wished that she could dredge up a little hardened hatred for him – just enough to prevent her from pining for something she knew she could never have.

She'd told him that she loved him. She could still picture his look of utter shock when she'd said the words. He hadn't said it back, but she swore that she could feel that he returned the sentiment. At the time, they'd been alone. Their friends – the small group who they'd hung around with – were nowhere to be seen. She'd felt moved to confide her feelings for him in a moment when he was being particularly loving and tender towards her.

He hadn't always been tender. Sometimes – especially when there was another pretty girl in the vicinity – he would ignore her. Sometimes, he would out and out blank her. She always forgave him because she'd believed that she understood him.

Louis was a complicated character. He could appear so vulnerable and loving, and – at other times – selfish and arrogant. She made allowances for him. Life wasn't easy. She recognised that – in spite of his privileged background she saw him as lonely and insecure.

Bravado was what seemed to keep him afloat - that, and what she'd always believed was her love for him. He'd needed her. He'd said as much with the looks he'd shared with her when they'd been alone, and by the way he would cling to her whenever he'd had a particularly bad meeting with his mother. He'd once told her that she was his rock.

It hadn't mattered that he couldn't find the words to tell her that he loved her. She *felt* loved. Even when he was being an ass, she still felt that he cared just as deeply for her as she did for him.

They'd been too young – she saw that now. They'd come together as a couple before he had truly come into his own. He hadn't been ready for what she had to offer.

But was he ready now?

She seriously doubted it. Ten years might have passed - and he'd grown up a great deal in that time – but most of the time, he was still an ass. He still treated women as if they were a commodity.

He'd told her that he didn't want to marry anyone but her. She still didn't understand why. Something buried deep inside her consciousness suggested that it was because he remembered his long-ago unspoken feelings for her.

She couldn't allow herself to believe that. All roads coming off the back of that would surely lead to ruin.

Why was he so upset about Robert? She couldn't shake the question. He'd reacted like a jealous lover.

Something was seriously wrong with the whole situation. Something was seriously wrong with *him*.

She began to imagine that she could fix him. She began to believe that she could make him love her. If she married him, she could awaken that precious thing inside of him that would make him truly need her. She could open him up to the very possibility of love. It wasn't an impossibility. He liked her. She even thought – the Robert lie notwithstanding – that he respected her. Love could blossom from like and respect. She was sure of it.

But, what about the other women? She knew that he could never promise to be faithful. Could she bear living with that – with knowing that he sought relief from his passions in the arms of others?

She thought not.

Then again...

She loved him, and she suddenly found herself terrified of losing what chance she had to have him.

She wanted to see that tender look in his eyes again. She wanted to melt against him and feel his arms around her. To have the chance of that – even if it meant sharing him – was becoming increasingly tempting.

Self-disgust washed over her. She was a disgrace to her sex. Had she no pride?

Her mother had a direct line to the queen. She decided that she would ask her to use it.

Downstairs, moments later, she accepted her mother's anger with a stoic resignation. The news that she'd denied the queen's request to meet with her didn't go down well. She appeased her with the promise that she'd meet with Louis to discuss his marriage proposal. She wanted her mother to convey that to the queen and to set up a meeting.

'You're doing the right thing,' she said, relief making her body sag. 'I'm glad that you've seen sense.'

Felicity didn't think that she'd seen sense. She thought that she'd actually lost the last vestige of it, but she had come to realise that she couldn't fight what her heart was commanding her to do. As soon as she'd realised that she would have him at any cost, she was beat.

Chapter Fifteen

'It beggars belief, Felicity.' Alice shook her head in bewilderment. 'I mean... you're really going to discuss marriage with him... after all you said before?' She shook her head once more. 'Do you remember the *over my dead body* remark?'

Felicity peered at her over the edge of her glass. She wasn't sure why her friend was acting so shocked. Alice had been emphatic in her efforts to get her to accept Louis' proposal in the first place, and now she seemed to be attempting to persuade her to give up on the whole idea of being his wife.

'I remember it, yes,' she said. 'A girl can change her mind, can't she?'

'But, why? What's caused this complete about face?'

She shrugged. 'I just think it's the right thing to do.'

'Really?' She voiced a *huh* sound. 'I wish you'd tell me where the real Felicity has disappeared to, because the one sitting in front of me sure isn't her.'

'I thought you'd approve.'

'Yes, of a rational decision... not this absurd *it's the right thing to do* nonsense.'

Felicity had nearly lost her nerve several times since asking her mother to set up a meeting with Louis. Her prevarication was one of the reasons she'd asked her mother to do it, instead of ringing Louis directly and arranging it herself. She'd thought – if she heard his voice – she'd chicken out. With her shock, and her questions, Alice was now forcing her to think again about her decision.

'I didn't really mean it,' Alice said. 'I didn't want you to take me seriously.'

'Nothing you said brought me to this decision, Alice, so stop worrying. I made up my own mind.'

'But are you sure?'

She hesitated, and Alice pounced. 'You're not, are you? I knew it. You've been brainwashed by your mother.'

'No, I'm not sure – not one hundred percent, but whoever is?'

'People in love, Felicity... people *in love* are sure.'

I am in love. 'I won't be truly sure until I talk to him again.'

'And when is that likely to be?'

'Tomorrow.'

She huffed out a sigh. 'I just don't get it.'

Felicity closed her eyes . There was a pain behind them. She needed to be honest with someone – share everything and unload the weight of dread from off her chest – but she wasn't convinced that Alice was the best person to confide in.

She felt her friend's cool hand on hers and blinked her eyes open.

'You look tortured,' she said. 'Are you sure that you're not being forced into this?'

'I'm not being forced, no... not in the way you think.'

'In what way, then?'

Felicity saw the earnest, almost frightened look in her friend's eyes and realised that Alice was *exactly* the right person to confide in. She may be a tittle-tattle, and she may be scatter-brained at the best of times, but Alice loved her. She would never hurt her or steer her wrong.

'If I tell you,' she began, grabbing hold of Alice's hand and holding on for dear life. 'If I tell you, do you promise to keep it to yourself?'

Alice coloured. She knew what Felicity was implying. She wasn't good at keeping secrets.

'I promise,' she said. 'I'll keep my mouth shut this time.'

'Okay.' She loosened her grip on Alice's hand, sat back, and gave a relieved moan. 'It's really quite simple.' Alice shifted forward. 'I've loved him constantly... persistently... madly... for over ten years. I don't care about my pride, or my self-esteem, or the fact that he'll probably end up ripping my heart out with his bare hands.' She hitched in a breath. 'I thought that I'd be okay. I thought that refusing him would somehow make me whole, but I now know that I can never be whole without him.'

'Oh, Felicity.' Alice shuffled out of her seat, went around the table, and hunkered down, placing both hands on Felicity's knees. 'You poor thing,' she said. 'All this time...?'

She nodded and stifled a sob. 'Pathetic, huh?'

'No, don't be silly. You can't help who you love.'

'I should have more pride than this.'

'Pride takes a hike in these situations, but you need to take a breath, honey. You need to really think about what you might be letting yourself in for.'

'I *have* thought about it,' she said. 'I've thought of nothing else.'

'Do you think that you can be honest with him?'

'You mean – tell him how I feel?' She threw her head violently from side to side. 'I'd rather die.'

Alice had no words. With an expression of baleful apprehension, she opened and closed her mouth. Her anxiety for her friend spilled over as she struggled to find the words to help her see sense, and she finally found her voice.

'What do you see happening here? Are you prepared to sacrifice yourself, your future, your whole bloomin' life, Felicity - and all for a few snippets of time with a man who wants to use you? Because – and I know this for a fact – he'll marry you and then he'll abandon you. It's his nature. He's just like his father.'

'He can be kind,' she replied defensively.

'Kind?' Alice snorted. 'Kind can only go so far. You want a man who loves you.'

'You've changed your tune.' She knew that Alice was only trying to help - to reason with her – but she was beginning to wish that she hadn't said anything. The trouble was – she was right. She didn't know what she'd wanted from her friend but pointing out the ugly truth wasn't it.

'I know I can say stupid things,' Alice returned. 'What I said before... in the café... I wasn't thinking.'

Felicity wanted to leave. She'd had enough. Confiding in Alice had left her feeling more miserable than ever. She'd thought that she had it all worked out – agree to marry Louis, turn a blind eye to any extramarital affairs, live with him and love him, and push to one side the fact that she wasn't loved in return.

It was completely insane.

She didn't care. Regardless of anything her friend said, she was doing it.

That revelation made her feel slightly better. She dragged in a breath and let it out slowly. The decision was made, and the relief was overwhelming.

'You're actually going to do it, aren't you?' Alice got back to her feet and stepped back to her chair. She plonked herself down heavily. 'Well, I wish you all the luck in the world. I hope you don't live to regret it.'

She took a slug of her wine, her hand shaking and almost spilling it. She laughed. It saved her from crying. She suddenly felt all of a tremble. She'd really made her mind up. She had no more doubts. The terror the decision evoked was all-consuming.

She was really going to do it.

'Will you be one of my bridesmaids?'

'What?' Alice nearly choked on her own mouthful of wine. 'You mean it?'

'Of course. You're my best friend.'

'If I said *yes*, it would seem like I'm condoning it.'

'If you said *yes*, it would be to support me. Even if you think that I'm making a terrible mistake, you should be there for me, Alice. I need you.'

She thought about it for all of a nanosecond. 'Of course, I'd be honoured.'

'Right, then. It's settled.'

Chapter Sixteen

L ouis could only describe it as a council of war or – at best – a trial. His mother sat - straight-backed and solemn - at the head of the table, his father on her left, and the imbecile Horace on her right. He sat further down, the space between them like a yawning maw.

Since the evening of his mother's dinner party, things had changed. The devastation seen on his father's normally indifferent face spoke volumes. He'd been told of the queen's terminal illness, and – although the news had been shared days before – he was still reeling from it.

Horace knew. Horace had always known because nothing ever escaped him. When he looked at Louis, his expression remained passively aggressive. Louis wondered why the private secretary had a seat at the table. What they were discussing was none of his business, and he'd said as much – only to be silenced by the look in his mother's eyes.

She didn't look well. Although she sat ramrod-straight, there was a weariness to her posture that suggested she was fighting the desire to simply flop. He wanted to go to her, to put his arms around her, and give her comfort, but he knew that was the last thing she'd want from him. The only thing she wanted was a resolution to the marriage question. She wanted him to agree to the name she'd put forward. Felicity's apology had fallen on deaf ears, and – as far as the queen was concerned – she was out of the running. The only woman she now wanted him to marry was the Lady Constance Archer – a woman Louis barely knew.

Louis had refused. He'd attempted to qualify his refusal with sharing his belief that the public wouldn't be fooled into believing it was a love-match. He'd never been seen with her. He'd never made mention of her. She was, to all intents and purposes, a stranger to him, and the people would know that. He'd asked to meet with his parents to put the case for Felicity. Before he met her, at her request, and before he put the question to her for a final time, he needed his mother's approval.

She wasn't intent on giving it.

They'd been going around in circles for what seemed like hours. His mother wasn't convinced that the public would be any more fooled by his marriage to Felicity than to Constance. He'd countered with the fact that he had a history with Felicity – a history that was well known – and that they were also known to move in the same circles. She'd been to the birthday dinner – an occurrence that could only be seen as a rubber-stamping of her place in the queen's affection. Her mother was one of the queen's closest friends, and – to cap it all – she'd pretty much grown up at Louis' heels.

'There remains the issue of her affair with a married man,' Horace piped up during a period of lengthy silence. 'The newspapers would have a field day.'

'She denies the affair,' Louis retorted, with more than a touch of irritation. 'And anyway – I'm hardly the epitome of propriety - not when it comes to disastrous love affairs. Why would the media go after her when I've proven myself to be less than moral?'

'It's always different for women,' his mother said. 'The future queen must be beyond reproach.'

'If I don't have a problem with it, I don't see why anyone else should.'

'Is it still going on… the affair?' his father asked.

'I told you – she denies it.'

'Do you believe her?'

He wasn't sure how to answer that. He decided to be economical with the truth. 'She's not seeing him at all now. He's out of the picture.'

From Horace - 'Well, that's something, at least.'

'I'm still very disappointed in her,' the queen said. 'She had an opportunity to explain herself to me, and she refused.'

Louis sighed and ran a hand wearily through his hair. 'How many times do you expect her to apologise for that, mother? Sometimes, you simply have to forgive, and move on.'

'Don't speak to Her Majesty like that,' Horace snapped, his face stretching with a scowl.

'Oh, shut up, Horace,' he snapped back. 'You shouldn't even have a voice at this table.'

He looked as if he was chewing a wasp. His mouth worked malevolently, and his eyes bored hatred into Louis' face, but he dropped into silence. It was a reluctant silence, because he believed that he was entitled to speak his mind, but he also knew the sense in biding his time.

'Look, mother, we like each other,' Louis said. 'Surely, that's a better recipe for success than foisting a woman I hardly know onto me?'

Her eyes flickered. He saw that she was wavering. She may want his marriage to occur for her own reasons, but he also knew that she wanted it to work out long-term. She wasn't being entirely selfish in pushing for a wedding before she died. She was trying to set a foundation for the future of her country.

It was time for an ultimatum. They wouldn't like it. None of them sitting at the other end of the table would accept it, but he was going to insist that they do, or they could forget him ever marrying.

'I'm going to agree to meet with her,' he said. 'I'm going to ask her to marry me again, and – if she refuses – I'll consider marrying Constance. But...' He eyed them individually, his eyes daring them to object. 'But, if she agrees, then you'll pull out all the stops to welcome her, and give her a wedding to remember, or I walk away from any and all discussions on marriage.'

He waited for the first of the objections to be voiced. His father glanced at his mother, but Horace kept his eyes fixed on him. No one spoke for what seemed like an eternity, then, his mother said, 'Very well.'

That was it – just, a curt *very well* – and it was suddenly, surprisingly, agreed. He blinked, believing he'd misheard.

'You agree?' He cleared his throat. 'I can give it one more go?'

'Yes, but you must promise to marry Constance if it all goes awry.'

She sounded different – almost defeated – and Louis felt a stab of guilt. He knew how important it was to her, and he'd effectively blackmailed her into acquiescing. He refused to feel ashamed of himself. He was a mere pawn on the chessboard that was the monarchy. One day, he may be the king, but – for now – he was being sacrificed for the sake of the queen. He was entitled to have his say in how he was to be sacrificed, and he refused to apologise for drawing a line in the sand.

He wanted Felicity. He was going to have Felicity. Nothing, and no one, was going to prevent it from happening. He knew that he would never have to deliver on his promise to marry Constance, because he was going to get his own way. This time, she would accept him. He was sure of it.

When they left the room, he sat at the table for long minutes, thinking. Although the queen had passed on Felicity's message, via her mother, for her request to see and speak to him, she'd did so with a reluctance that bordered on ferocity. He didn't think she would remain friends with Felicity's mother for very much longer. In his eyes, that wasn't necessarily a bad thing. The two women made a powerful alliance and, if his marriage to Felicity was to prove a successful one – in that there would be a minimum of fuss made about how they chose to co-habit – that alliance was best shattered.

He had no intention on toeing the moral high ground. The marriage would be one of convenience. He would have certain expectations, and he was mindful that Felicity would also expect certain things from him, but that didn't mean they would live conventionally. That would likely cause both mothers' eyebrows to be raised in consternation. Neither would be happy. He would be able to cope with Felicity's mother disapproving from a distance, but – if she remained close to his own mother – life could prove difficult.

He picked up his phone and stared at the screen. Could he really do this? Could he ring her, set the wheels in motion, and cast both their futures in concrete?

He brought up her number. His finger hovered over the little green button. He worried that he would end up condemning her to a life of duty and ultimate loneliness – much like his own had been all of his years.

He pressed it.

Chapter Seventeen

With his hands shoved deep into the pockets of his jacket, and with the fluid grace of a leopard, he made his way across the large patio towards her. He looked as if he didn't have a care in the world, and – watching him – Felicity felt her heart stutter in her chest. He had no right looking so absolutely perfect. It simply wasn't fair.

Despite her feelings, she feigned nonchalance, and tried to pay no heed to her burgeoning desire for a man who – as had become perfectly clear – was put on this Earth simply to torture her. It wasn't his fault – not all of it. He hadn't asked her to fall in love with him all those years before, and he certainly couldn't be blamed for the fact that she was still desperately infatuated with him. What he *could* be blamed for, was that he'd inserted himself back into her life, instead of giving her another few years to get over him.

She sat at the little patio table and casually sipped her wine - her heart ricocheting against her ribs, and her face expressionless. She had things to say, and she wanted them said in as emotionless a manner as possible. She was determined not to show, by word or action, how affected she was by him. She wasn't going to strip her emotions bare and leave herself wide-open to more pain. He wanted what was little more than a business arrangement with her. In return for a crown, she would marry him – or so he thought.

Being queen meant nothing to her. A life of untold privilege wasn't what tempted her into being on the cusp of saying yes to him.

Sitting there, and watching his graceful approach, she knew there was only one reason she wanted to marry him – she couldn't bear the thought of life without him. She'd thought that she could. She'd spent the last ten years believing that she could. Now, she knew different.

She was no longer the reluctant bride. Now, she wanted nothing more than to be his wife – no matter the cost.

Her eyes flicked over to the left. Her mother hovered in the doorway, watching. Felicity knew exactly what she was thinking. Her mother realised that everything now depended on how she reacted to the meeting with Louis. She almost felt sorry for her. She'd left her wondering. She'd refrained from confiding in her and had merely said that she was now willing to hear Louis out and consider his proposal. Her mother had absolutely no idea how she felt. A mother *should* know, she thought bitterly. Not for the first time, she felt the absence of a mother's arms, and a mother's soothing words of understanding.

She was exhausted. Two nights with barely any sleep had turned her brain to mush. The exhaustion actually heightened her emotional fragility, and – for a fleeting moment – she wondered if, in her current state, she should be making such a momentous decision. But, if she didn't, she didn't think she would ever sleep soundly again.

He closed the distance between them, stopped, and looked down at the top of her head. 'May I sit?' he asked.

She found his eyes. They looked troubled. 'Of course,' she said, then – on an afterthought – added, 'You look nice.'

She bit her tongue, sharply enough to make her wince. *What a stupid thing to have said.*

His mouth quirked. 'You look beautiful, as ever.' He sat. 'I'm glad you asked to see me. I wanted to apologise for my behaviour at mother's dinner.'

She wasn't expecting an apology. She didn't want one. All she wanted was to get down to the business of accepting his proposal.

'How about offering me a glass of wine?'

She pushed the bottle across the table. 'Help yourself.'

She looked across at her mother, raised an eyebrow, and stared at her until she turned and disappeared back inside the house.

He poured some wine into a glass, leaned back in the chair, and stretched out his long legs.

Felicity emptied the remaining wine into her own glass. She was ever so proud of the fact that her hand didn't tremble as she raised it to her lips.

A heavy silence descended. It seemed that neither of them was keen to break it. Strangely, the silence wasn't uncomfortable.

The minutes ticked by, and soft music suddenly danced in the air. Her mother was playing the piano in the music room and the melodious notes escaped through the open window.

'Do you play?'

Her head jerked up. 'What?'

'The piano? Do you play the piano?'

'Sometimes.'

'Are you any good?'

'My mother certainly wouldn't say so.'

'I never learned how. I sometimes play the guitar. When I was younger – before I first met you - I wanted to be in a rock band. That dream was soon knocked out of my head.'

She didn't know what to say to that.

'I've never been allowed to realise a single one of my dreams. I had one path, and woe betide me if I ever stumbled off it.' He looked at her through hooded eyes, watching for any sign that she was understanding the nuance of his words. 'Don't get me wrong – I strayed off it many times. Sometimes, I didn't care about the consequences.'

She didn't know why, but his words irked her. 'What's the point of this, Louis? Do you want me to feel sorry for you?'

'Good heavens, no.'

'Then, what?'

'It's just conversation, Felicity. Can't we simply sit and chat... share things about one another?'

'That's not why I asked to see you,' she said.

'I just thought...'

She raised a hand. 'Please, Louis... let's just get this over with.'

'Goodness, it sounds like you're about to get a limb removed without anaesthetic.'

He'd hit the nail on the head. That was *exactly* how she felt.

'Ask me,' she said.

He frowned. 'Ask you what?'

'Please...' Her voice was a mere whisper. 'Don't toy with me.'

The control on her emotions was slipping and slipping fast. He had to ask her, and she had to answer, quickly, so she could get away from him and come to better terms with her decision.

'Any chance of another bottle of wine?'

The question startled her. 'You need some Dutch courage?'

He nodded. 'I sure do.'

'Why?'

'Because I'm afraid of hearing your answer to *that* question.'

She tried to push his response away. Understanding what he meant might prove to be too much for her to handle. But her brain was much quicker than her feeble attempt to distance herself from what he might have meant.

He's not sure about any of this, her brain mutinously forced her to think. He might want her to refuse again. If she did refuse him, he might be quietly relieved.

'You remember that path I mentioned?'

'The one that you stray off of sometimes?'

'Yes, that one. Well – I'm just about to go scampering off it, and into very uncertain territory. I can't do that without more wine.'

'What do you mean?' She was afraid to hear his answer.

'Well, before I ask you again... and I *will* ask again... I've decided to share my reasons with you... confide in you. I think I know what your answer is going to be. I don't think you would've asked to see me if it was going to be more of the same. I'm not sure why you might've changed your mind but – whatever your reasons are – I think you deserve to know why I've chased you like a crazy loon these past weeks.'

She weighed everything up in her tumultuous mind. Curiosity got the better of her anxiety, and she nodded.

'Wait there. I'll be right back.'

She moved across the patio quickly and disappeared into the same door he'd emerged from not long before. Her heels clicked across the tiled floor as she headed for the kitchen. The music stopped. She ignored the sudden silence and refused to halt to turn to where she knew her mother would now be standing - waiting and demanding an explanation as to what was going on.

She entered the kitchen with a trace of a smile on her face. It felt good to leave her mother hanging. *Let her wonder*, she thought. *Let her worry and imagine that things aren't going the way she wanted them to.*

She grabbed two bottles of wine – one red and one white. She had a feeling that they were going to need both.

Despite her ongoing feelings of animosity and hurt towards her mother - on her way back across the wide hallway - she turned to look at her, albeit reluctantly.

'It's all right,' she said. 'We're not done talking.'

'Has he..?'

She shook her head. 'Not yet, but he says that he will.'

'When he asks... please say yes, Felicity.'

She shielded her thoughts. Her mother wasn't going to be told her answer before Louis heard it. It had to be their business before it became hers.

Louis sagged back in the chair. She emerged from the door, hugging the wine to her chest, and watched him for a moment before stepping back out and onto the patio.

He looked miles away – deep in thought, and perturbed.

Louis *was* perturbed. During her absence, he'd been wondering if the whole thing was utter folly. The thoughts weren't new. Hardly a day had gone by without him questioning everything in his mind. He knew that he could enter into a loveless marriage, and learn to live with it, but he worried that it could all be for nothing. The dissolution of the monarchy could still happen. A royal wedding, and a fresh wave of support from the public – might not make an iota of difference to the Prime Minister's plans. His mother might, very well, end up being the last reigning monarch.

Then, there was Felicity. He liked her. He couldn't and wouldn't deny that. What if, through time, she fell in love with someone else? Could he forbid her any hope of happiness? Was he that selfish? Did the possibility of inheriting the crown mean that much to him?

The questions reverberated around and around in his head. When she returned with the wine, he still had no answers.

The glug of the wine as it hit the side of the glass focussed his thoughts. He would be honest with her. It was the only way. She could make her own mind up and enter into a marriage – or not – with her eyes wide open.

He determined that this would be the very last time he would ever bring up the subject with her. If she said no, he would never see her again. If she said yes, then he hoped that she wouldn't live to regret it. He would try to be a faithful husband. He would try to ensure that she was the only woman he would ever be intimate with.

He gave an unconscious, rueful smile.

'What's so funny?' she asked, leaning over the table to take her re-filled glass.

'Funny?'

'You were smiling to yourself.'

'Was I?' He gave himself a mental shake. There certainly hadn't been anything amusing about his thoughts. The last one was – *Faithful*? *Who are you kidding*?

'Tell me,' she said.

'About what I was thinking?'

'No... the reason for pursuing me. The reason you have to marry me. You said that you would.'

'In a minute.' He took a long swallow of wine.

She waited, her eyes never leaving his face.

'You have to promise me something first,' he said. 'I can't tell you unless you promise.'

She thought about it, then nodded. 'All right... I'll give you my promise. What is it?'

'That the reason remains strictly between us. You have to promise not to tell anyone.'

That sounded simple enough. 'Okay.'

Sorry mother.

He told her everything.

Chapter Eighteen

Digesting his words took considerable effort on her part. What he told her both saddened and numbed her.

'Dying?' She shook her head. 'I can't quite believe it.'

He nodded. 'It does take quite a bit of getting used to, and to accept.'

'What about treatment? Surely..?'

'She's had a course of chemo, and radiotherapy. I still don't know how she managed to keep it a secret.'

'And all the worry about what the Prime Minister is up to.' Her eyes flashed. 'I could punch him on the nose.'

He gave a small chortle. 'I believe you would.'

'Too right, I would.'

The scent of her mother's roses and the lavender growing along one of the borders was in her nose. She closed her eyes. The scent had suddenly brought forth a sense of impending death – a funeral smell. She shuddered. Her mother would be devastated to lose her friend.

'I made some discreet enquiries, off my own bat, about what the PM is up to. Unfortunately, it's all true. He really means to get rid of us.' She saw that his eyes had deepened almost to black. 'My mother's death will just be the springboard he needs.'

'I can't believe that no one knows about her illness. How is that possible?'

'You know my mother - she can keep a secret better than anyone I've ever known.'

'How long does she have?'

He shrugged. 'Perhaps a year... no more, I don't think.'

Her back straightened and her eyes filled with tears.

'I'm so sorry.' Without thinking, she reached out for his hand. It felt cold, and she felt the faintest tremor in his fingers as they closed around hers. 'You must be devastated.'

'I thought I might have got used to it. I've known for a couple of weeks.'

'That's not long.'

'No, but...' He withdrew his hand. 'There's no point in me dwelling on it. It'll happen, whether I get into a state about it, or not.'

Now, everything made perfect sense. He needed a wife before his mother died. He needed a wife to attempt to save his birth right. He needed a wife because he wanted to grant his mother some peace of mind.

'Is it enough?'

'Of a reason?'

She felt like a fox caught in the headlights. She had been all set to agree to marry him. She'd discovered that she wanted to, more than anything, but now..? The doubts were rampaging around in her head. Marrying him would be a balm to his troubles. It would ease him – ease his worry about his mother, and his future. For a while, he would truly need her, and would welcome any comfort a marriage to her could offer. Instead of it making her rush to give him the answer he so desperately sought, the situation gave her pause for serious thought.

She said, 'It should be, but...'

'You still can't do it? You still can't accept my proposal?'

'I'm... I'm not sure. I have to take a moment to think.'

'I don't have many moments left, Felicity. Even if you said yes today, we'd be hard-pressed to pull a wedding off before... before... well, before she was too ill to attend, or she died.'

'I promise... only a moment. I just need a moment to gather my thoughts.' Her head was reeling. She pushed her glass away. She wouldn't drink any more. She said, 'We could do this, and I still might not be queen?'

'Would that matter?'

'No,' she said, truthfully.

'Marriage – a royal wedding – would give us a chance.'

'Yes, I see that.' She ran a hand across her eyes. She wished that he hadn't told her. If he'd remained quiet – kept the queen's secrets – he would already have had her answer.

'Does your mother want me for you? Would I be *her* choice?'

'I think so. I know she's threatened me with a selection of other suitable young women – one in particular – but I think she likes you. She thinks you'll be good for me, and that you'll make a strong consort.'

'She was very angry at me for refusing to meet with her. My mother told me just how angry she was.'

'She got over it.'

'Does she know that you're here?'

He nodded.

Confusion worked at her heart and mind. What had once seemed so uncomplicated, was now riddled with conundrum. She loved him, so she would marry him – that had been her decision. Was it still her decision?

'Okay,' she said.

He paled. She actually witnessed the blood drain from his face.

'Are you sure?' he squeezed out, hardly believing what she'd just said. 'Really, Felicity?'

'I'm as sure as I can be.' She felt the colour drain from her own cheeks. 'Just don't hurt me, Louis.'

He stared at her long and hard, then brushed a finger along the length of her arm.

She shivered. 'Please,' she said. 'Please, don't.'

He raised his finger and stroked her lips. 'It would be a real marriage, Felicity. I don't want you to be in any doubt about that. I won't go into this half-heartedly.'

Her lips parted. They burned beneath his touch. She stopped breathing.

'I would want to be a proper husband. I'd make love to you, do you understand?'

His eyes darkened and she found herself being drawn into them. His honesty was unsettling. How would she bear sharing a bed with him, feeling his body cover hers, knowing he didn't love her?

She nodded and, before she knew what was happening, his mouth took possession of her.

It was over much too quickly, and then he was simply staring at her once more.

'Thank you,' he said.

She looked at him in consternation. Gone was the arrogant slant to his features, the assured cast in his eye. Before her was simply a man, not a prince, and he seemed genuinely touched and grateful.

'You're welcome,' she said. 'Now, what?'

'Now?' He leaned forward. 'Now, I want to kiss you again.'

That kiss removed any lasting doubts she had about how she felt about him. She loved him – loved him far more than she'd ever did as a besotted eighteen-year-old girl. It was a much harder, more painful love. It was a mature love that couldn't be assuaged by any feelings of hate that she still harboured for how he'd treated her. It was the sort of love that could quite easily destroy her.

After he withdrew his lips that second time, she realised that she would hate every minute of walking up the aisle in whatever cathedral they'd choose for the wedding. She knew that saying her vows would most probably choke her, but she would do it regardless. She would hold her head high and say the words that would bind her to him forever. She would say them reluctantly, miserably. She would promise him the Earth in those vows and listen as he did the same.

She would keep her promises to him, but she knew that he wouldn't keep his. It would be an impossibility for him, but she'd still take him, she'd still love him.

That kiss – that damned kiss – had been her utter undoing.

Chapter Nineteen

Their first date as a couple was planned with military precision. Louis had suggested something low-key, but the full weight of the queen's opinion overrode his wish for as little fuss as possible. His mother wanted – if not fanfare – at least some significant media attention. She hoped that them being seen together at a high-profile event would create a beginning to the gossip that would ultimately have everyone anticipating a proper royal romance. She also hoped it would end the incessant speculation about her son's erratic love-life.

She reminded him of how little time they had. She reinforced the need to move quickly with their public courtship, and to announce their engagement within weeks.

Felicity was already being groomed. Even before she had stepped out on his arm, for the world to see, she was being shaped and formed into the perfect princess. There were so many rules, protocols, and behaviours that were absolutely forbidden. She had to walk a certain way, climb in and out of a car a certain way, dress a certain way. There were topics of conversation that she was denied engagement in. There had to be no mention of her previous job, and certainly no whisper of the trouble Robert had caused with his lie – not that anyone believed it to be a lie. Louis didn't refer to it, but she knew he continued to harbour the belief that she'd been his lover.

Fortunately, she had a good insight into the various duties associated with her role. Her upbringing – with a mother who'd instilled in her the need to keep a close eye on what went on in royal circles – meant that she'd been spoon-fed such details her whole life. That didn't mean that she was prepared enough to understand the rigours of those duties, and – if the planning and execution of their first date was anything to go on – she worried that she'd neither have the constitution, nor the desire, to take on such a rigorous job. Because, when all was said and done, it *was* a job – a twenty-four hour, seven days a week job.

The high-profile event was the wedding of one of Louis' cousins. Arriving on his arm at that well-publicised event would set the cat amongst the pigeons. No one would be left in any doubt that their new relationship was serious.

The queen said that this was the one occasion when a guest was allowed to upstage the bride. She said it without a modicum of guilt or embarrassment and insisted that she had complete sway over what Felicity would wear.

Felicity was ready to have a melt-down. Everything was happening much too fast. Louis took both of her hands in his and smiled solemnly into her face. For once, his mother had made herself scarce, and they had a moment alone.

'Take a breath,' he said. 'If you don't like the outfit she chose for you, then don't wear it. If you don't want to attend the wedding with me, then cry off. Whatever you want... however you want to play it... that's fine with me.'

She was at a loss for words. He'd been an absolute angel since she'd accepted his proposal, and – now that he was taking her side against his mother – she didn't know what to say to show him how grateful she was.

His grip on her hands tightened. 'Don't be afraid to stand up for yourself, Felicity. You hold all the power here.'

'It doesn't feel like it,' she replied, on a moan. 'The queen is a very formidable woman... even more formidable than my mother, and that's saying something.'

'The two of them make quite the tag-team.'

'Tell me about it. Yesterday – and the day before, come to that – they both ganged up on me about my friendship with Alice. They want me to end it. You should've seen the look on their faces when I told them that she was going to be my maid of honour.'

She smiled through her anxiety. Louis didn't seem shocked. He knew and liked Alice, and she was sure that he'd be in her corner when it came to her insisting on her friend being front and centre at the nuptials.

'Whatever you want, love. I'll add my voice to the argument if needs be.'

She grew more and more in love with him with each passing day. So far, he'd been the perfect gentleman, and was delivering on his promise not to hurt her. She even thought that he'd dumped all of the female hangers-on who he'd been frequently seen with out and about town. The sensible part of her brain refused to allow her to imagine that he was falling in love with her, but her heart believed in the possibility. She never, for a moment, thought it was all a ruse to keep her sweet, and to prevent her from having second thoughts.

'Have you chosen your best man?' she asked.

'I definitely know who it's going to be, and my choice will cause just as much of a ruckus as your maid of honour.'

'Is it Jacob?'

'Yes, it's Jacob.'

'Why would anyone object to him?'

'He's not family.'

'Why would that matter?'

'Tradition.' He moved away and sat down on a chair by the window.

They were in one of the small sitting rooms in the private residence at the palace. It was a lovely room. It was Felicity's most favourite room in the whole place. She felt comfortable because it was an unpretentious space, and everyone had accepted it as her and Louis' domain, so they were often left alone there.

It took a valiant effort for her not to follow him across the room and plonk herself in his lap. They hadn't gone down the route of displays of affection. Apart from those two small kisses a week before, Louis hadn't shown anything other than gentle concern, and occasional handholding.

She couldn't deny that she wanted him. She dreamt about making love to him every night when she went to sleep and woke up every morning with a feeling of despair when she'd realised it hadn't been real.

They hadn't spoken about it – not since he'd made it clear what he expected from the marriage. She wondered if, after they were officially engaged, if he'd touch her, and hold her, and kiss her again.

She hoped so.

'I like Jacob,' she said.

'And I like Alice,' he returned.

'So – you'll have him, and I'll have her?'

'Agreed.'

'And I can choose my own outfit for your cousin's wedding?'

'Of course.'

She sighed. 'Thank goodness for that. The dress and matching coat your mother chose for me is absolutely hideous. And the hat...' She threw her head back and laughed. 'I don't know what she was thinking with the hat.'

'She wants you to stand out.'

'Well, bright pink would certainly do that.'

'Sky blue suits you,' he said.

'What?' She screwed up her eyes.

'I said...'

'I know what you said, but... sky blue? Really?'

He shrugged. 'I like the way it makes your skin look luminous, and your eyes spark.'

'It's a bit insipid.'

'You're vibrant enough to stand it.'

Their eyes locked. He was the first to look away.

'Okay,' she said. 'I'll look for something in that colour.'

'Only if it's what you want.'

'We'll see.' She strolled over and looked down on him. 'Thank you,' she said. 'For everything. You've been such a rock.'

'Thank me later... when we've both survived our baptism by fire.'

'The wedding?'

He nodded. 'I have a feeling it's going to turn into a circus. I really feel for my cousin and his bride. They'll end up wishing they'd never invited me.'

'They'll understand.'

'Would you?'

'No, I guess not.' She thought a moment. 'Why don't we cancel?'

'Not go... either of us?'

'Well, *you* could go. It's only right that you do, but I could stay away... for their sakes.'

He grinned. 'We could decide on something else for our first official date.'

'What do you have in mind?'

'Something both of our mothers would abhor. It would show them we mean business, and that they've to back off.'

'A night club?'

'There's a new one opening in Soho.'

'Sounds perfect.'

'Tonight?'

She swallowed and nodded.

'I'll see if Jacob and Patricia are free. We could go out as a foursome.'

'Even better.'

'How about asking Alice along?'

'She'd have to bring someone.'

'That would be okay.'

They were both excited. It was a wonderful feeling to finally take charge of their own lives – even if it was just for one night.

Chapter Twenty

The *Moonlight* sign was a riot of colour. It was tacky and that tackiness gave it a certain contradictory sophistication. The queue outside its garish red doors stretched like an anaconda for almost a mile. Entrance was by invitation only, but only a select few were allowed in. The others had to wait until the guest of honour arrived.

The press had got wind that Louis was attending the opening night, and the paparazzi were out in force. Traffic up and down the main road was chaotic, and more than one photographer almost found themselves under the wheels of one vehicle or another as they scrambled and jostled for position.

It was a warm night. The sun had long ago dipped below the horizon, and the streetlights were now popping on in waves, casting a yellow glow across the assembled crowd. There was no sign of Louis' car, and everyone was becoming restive.

Alice, and her boyfriend of the moment, arrived ahead of Louis' car. Louis' protection detail was almost bumper to bumper with Louis, and Jacob and Patricia followed their car in a taxi. It was quite a procession, and necks craned, and cameras clicked as every door opened in unison, and everyone emerged onto the pavement.

Felicity trembled with fright as a surge of reporters moved like a giant wave towards them, but Louis – being a dab hand at avoiding being trampled –held onto her around the waist and elbowed and pushed his way forward, ably assisted by the two burly officers on either side. The huge red doors swung open and soon swallowed them up.

Once inside, the noise hit them like an array of mortar shells. The music literally made the air bounce. Although it was fairly early in the evening – only just gone ten o'clock - and although there were hundreds of people queuing outside, there hardly seemed room enough to move.

Felicity was already thinking that the trip to the night-club was a bad idea. Louis, on the other hand, was in his element. He was a party animal. He loved the people, the music, and the manic atmosphere. He knuckle-bumped a few of the young men they passed, slapped one on the back, and grinned wolfishly at a few of the pretty women pressing close to him.

After ten minutes, Felicity wanted to leave. Alice – thoroughly enjoying herself, and the attention – told her she was stupid and to chill out and relax.

To give Louis his due, he never left her side, and clung onto her the whole night. They could hardly hear themselves talk, and so there was very little conversation. She watched him in action and, as every hour passed, she grew more and more convinced that he'd chosen the wrong woman when he'd chosen her. They were so obviously very different people.

A little after one o'clock, he'd had enough of standing on the sidelines, and dragged her onto the dancefloor. He was a great mover – sexy, unabashed, and had a rhythm that caused all eyes to follow him. That meant that all eyes were obviously on felicity, too. She could dance, and she wasn't normally self-conscious, but – being in his arms, with every eye in the club on them – caused her to be more than a little reticent. Louis was having none of that, and dragged her tightly against him, so her body was moulded to his, and forced her to match his every swaying, rhythmic move.

The music was fast and furious, but Louis moved at his own pace. It should've looked ridiculous, but – as was reported in the morning newspapers, and across social media – he *owned* that dancefloor.

Sweating, his hair slicked back off his face, he finally succumbed to her pleas for mercy, and walked her to a quieter spot at the bar to the rear of the club. They were alone for a few precious minutes before they were joined by the others in their group, and she took the opportunity to make the point that she felt like she was cramping his style.

'Nonsense,' he said into her ear. 'I'm enjoying myself so much because you're here with me.'

'Well, you're certainly having fun,' she returned a little waspishly. Jealousy was the main trigger for her current mood. Nearly every woman in the place had tried to grab his attention. He didn't brush off a single one of them, and that made her mad. It brought home to her just what she was taking on.

'What's wrong?' he asked, his lips brushing her ear. 'Aren't you enjoying yourself?'

She shook her head and turned away from him. He put his finger under her chin and forced her head back around to look at him.

'What?' he mouthed.

She shrugged, embarrassed by the green-eyed monster sitting on her shoulder.

He drew her against his chest and kissed the top of her head. It was his way of reassuring her. He wasn't stupid. He knew what she was thinking.

'I'm not interested in any of them,' he said.

She pushed back and looked up at him. 'They all want a piece of you. It's as if they believe they have a right to touch you, to make moony eyes at you.'

He laughed, amused by the fire in her eyes. Deep down, he was pleased that she was so affected by the attention paid to him. He didn't want her to be indifferent.

Alice arrived, huffing, and spent. 'I need a drink,' she said. Her date was soon at her elbow and caught the attention of the barman. He ordered two bottles of champagne and half a dozen glasses.

Jacob staggered over, held up by a rather furious Patricia, and all six leaned on the bar and caught their breaths.

'We're heading home in a minute,' Patricia said. 'My man has had more than enough fun for one night.'

Louis took Jacob into a huge bear-hug. 'Thanks, man,' he said. 'Thanks for coming.' He then draped an arm over Felicity's shoulder and dropped his mouth to plant a kiss on her neck.

A photographer just happened to be there at that precise moment, and that photograph found its way around the world before anyone had had their first cup of morning coffee.

'Just one more dance, and then we'll get off,' Louis said, grabbing Felicity's hand and dragging her back towards the dancefloor.

It was unusual to have a slow dance at a night-club, but there was an exception being played out when they climbed up the single step and onto the floor. An old song was playing – Chris De Burgh's *Lady in Red*. It was so apt, it was eerie. Felicity was wearing a red sheath dress.

She felt his heart hammering as he drew her into the circle of his arms. Her own heart was in her mouth as he pulled her close and made himself one with her. For the few minutes of the song, she was oblivious to everything but the smell and the feel of him.

'Did you request that song?' she asked as they climbed into the back of the protection detail's car ten minutes later.

He grinned and nodded. 'I wanted to end the night showing everyone that you're my girl.'

'I'm your girl? She grinned back at him.

'I'm marrying you, aren't I?'

Her grin wilted. 'That doesn't mean what it should, Louis,' she replied, soberly. 'We're not a normal couple, and our marriage won't be a conventional one.'

'I know that, but so what?'

'So, don't pretend. It's all right to put a show on for others, but - when it's just the two of us - let's be honest with one another.'

His face fell. 'I'm not pretending, Felicity. I like you. You know that. What's wrong with showing you just how much I like you?'

'It'll muddy the waters.'

'*Muddy the...* what are you on about?'

He didn't know how she felt about him, so she understood his confusion. He believed that it was perfectly all right to have an affection for one another. He didn't realise how much it hurt her to have that, and no more.

'Forget I said anything.' She wrapped her arms around herself and bowed her head. 'It was a lovely night,' she said. 'I ended up really enjoying it, and thanks for the last dance. It was very sweet of you.'

'I've never been called *sweet* before. It sounds almost like an insult.' He grabbed her hand. 'I'm glad you had a fun night. It did what we needed it to do, and we'll be the talk of the whole world with everyone wondering who you are, and what you mean to me.'

The car pulled to the kerb. She was home.

'Can I come in for a coffee?' he asked, his eyes narrowing ever so slightly.

She wanted to nod and say yes, but that was one step too many after him professing his *liking* for her. She knew what the coffee would lead to, and – although she wanted it – she wasn't ready for it.

'Perhaps another time,' she said. 'I'm tired.'

He was disappointed. She could clearly see that, but she wasn't swayed. She knew that she would hate herself in the morning if she surrendered to the want in his eyes.

'I'll see you tomorrow, then,' he said, opening the door. 'We're expected for lunch with the queen.'

She nodded and climbed from the car. He followed, and they stood staring at one another for long moments before he pecked her on the cheek and watched as she made her way to the front door.

She stood on the top step and looked back at him. He was still watching after her. He didn't get back into the car until she'd stepped inside and closed the door.

Chapter Twenty-One

'It's beautiful... absolutely breath-taking.' Felicity held out her hand and admired the ring under the overhead chandelier. 'Are those really all diamonds?'

'Every single one of them,' Louis replied, a huge grin on his face. 'It was my great-grandmother's engagement ring. I chose it especially.'

'Why this one? Why this ring?'

'Because it's a happy ring,' he said. 'My great-grandmother was a very happy woman... a very happy wife. I thought her ring would make her happiness rub off on you.'

Her face immediately sobered. She dropped her hand and allowed her arm to hang at her side. 'What makes you think that I'm not already happy?'

'Because your smiles never reach your eyes.'

'Nonsense. I'm perfectly happy, Louis,' she lied. 'Why wouldn't I be?'

He shrugged. 'If you'd prefer another ring, I can...'

'Don't be silly. It's perfect. It doesn't even need adjusting.'

'I'm sorry that I couldn't simply take you to a jewellery store and let you choose... like a normal couple.'

'We're not a normal couple, so your point is moot. Let's just pretend that none of that matters.'

'I'm not great at pretending.'

'That's a lie, for a start. You're the *great pretender*, Louis. You can't *pretend* that you're not.'

He was on the back foot, again. He still couldn't believe how much she knew about him. It was surreal.

'I'll not pretend around you,' he said. 'I'll always be honest... never lie.'

'Oh, but I want you to lie, Louis. I *need* you to lie.'

Shocked, he said, 'Whatever for?'

'To make it bearable.'

'Oh, God, Felicity... is this all so very terrible?'

'No,' she said, honestly. 'But I'm worried that it might *get* terrible. If you're always straight with me, I won't cope. So, I think there will be some things I'd rather you weren't honest about.'

'Such as?'

Her face flamed with colour.

'Oh.' He dropped his head. 'Right.' He shuffled from one foot to the other. 'You don't trust me.'

'No.'

'Well, that was blunt.'

'There was no other way to say it.'

He looked pained. 'I won't hurt you.'

'You might think you mean that, but...' She looked him straight in the eye. 'You won't be able to help yourself.'

'And you'll still marry me... knowing that?'

'Yes.'

'Then, you're a fool, Felicity. Forget everything. We haven't announced the engagement yet. Walk away. I won't hold it against you.'

'No.'

He growled in the back of his throat and advanced towards her. Gripping her shoulders, and feeling her tremble, he dragged her against his chest. 'I should never have forced you into this,' he said, pressing his mouth against her hair. 'It wasn't fair.'

'You didn't force me. I agreed to marry you because it's what I want.'

They were in his apartment at the palace, just minutes away from formally sharing their news to the world, and both of them were struggling with the consequences of their decision. He felt guilt begin to eat away at his determination to go ahead, and she was already worrying about how much she knew he was going to end up hurting her.

'I don't think I'll ever be able to lie to you,' he said, pulling her even closer. 'Anyway, you'd see right through any lie I tried to give.'

'You're not the only one who can pretend. I pretend to myself all the time. I'm quite capable of pretending that your lies are the truth.'

That gave him pause. She was so cool about it all. Her eyes were well and truly wide open, and he was amazed at her aplomb. What other woman would be so accepting of him?

No other woman, he thought. Only Felicity.

'I wish I could tell you that I loved you.' There was heartbreak in his voice. 'It's not that I don't want to... I simply can't feel it.'

'I know. It's all right.'

'I like you more than any other woman. I think I told you that once before?'

'You did. I remember.' She snaked her arms around his neck and pushed her head back so she could look at him. 'Why don't we go and get this over with?'

'It'll be a circus.'

She smiled. 'As long as you're at my side, I'll be all right.'

'Always, Felicity. I'll always be there for you... no matter what.'

'Another promise?'

'I'll keep this one.'

She tilted her head to the side and cocked a brow. 'You promise?'

He laughed. She really was quite amazing.

'That's better.'

'What is?'

'I don't like seeing you all serious.'

'You prefer the clown prince?'

'No, but a serious face doesn't suit you.'

'I'll have to remember that.' He pecked the tip of her nose. 'We'd better go.'

Outside of his embrace, she felt cold. He had a habit of hugging her. She was surprised at that – surprised at the ease in which he could hold her close, kiss her, be with her. Sometimes it almost felt as if they were a normal couple, in love, and looking forward to their wedding and a life together. Sometimes it was very easy to forget that nothing was true, that nothing was real.

The press conference was being held in the White Drawing Room. It was the grandest of all the state rooms at the palace, and this was the first time that a press conference had been held there.

Louis had chosen it as the venue to break the news. It wasn't the only one of his decisions that his mother took exception to. It seemed that nothing he suggested met with her approval, but – as with every other decision he'd made around the whole wedding situation – he stuck to his guns, and she was forced to acquiesce.

He stood with his arm around Felicity's shoulders, in front of the portrait of Queen Alexandra, and faced the cameras and the reporters with a quiet dignity. The time had come to take the most important step in their plan, and he suddenly found that he was rather anxious.

He worried that they would see right through him. He worried that he would fumble his words and show the world just how much of a fraud he was. The public believed that he was marrying the love of his life. They expected to see a certain emotion in his eyes, and he feared that he would blow it.

He knew that Felicity was just as nervous. He wasn't to know that, when she looked at him, and when the cameras captured that look, no one would be left in any doubt about how *she* felt about *him*.

As usual, she looked stunning. He was very proud to have her next to him. She'd already proven herself to be a worthy partner, and he couldn't help but congratulate himself for his wise choice.

So far, she hadn't put a foot wrong. She was always poised, attentive, and well informed whenever he'd introduced her to people of importance, or when he escorted her to official functions. Even though they hadn't confirmed their legitimate relationship until today, the fact that he'd been almost glued to her side for weeks had painted the picture they'd wanted.

Now, it was time to rubber-stamp everything with a presentation of the ring, and a few words outlining their marriage plans.

They would be surprised – even shocked – when they discovered just how soon the wedding would take place. It was being planned in unprecedented haste, and eyebrows were sure to be raised.

'How long have you known one another?' one reporter asked.

'Oh, for absolutely ages,' Louis replied. 'Actually, since we were children.'

'Have you always loved her?'

He glanced down at her. 'Always,' he said.

'You dated a few years ago. Why did you break up?'

'We were too young,' Felicity returned. 'But I always knew he was the man for me.'

A perfect answer, Louis thought. *She was really good at this.*

'You said that the wedding will be in four months. Why the rush?'

'Because I can't wait,' she threw out with a smile. 'The date is convenient to Her Majesty, so why not?'

There was a bubble of laughter around the room. She had everyone eating out the palm of her hand.

'Hold your hand up,' someone called out. 'Let's see the ring.'

Cameras clicked. The beauty of the ring was now immortalised on her finger.

The headlines would scream – *a couple in love*. Everyone had been fooled.

Chapter Twenty-Two

He had no sense of trouble ahead. Everything was going swimmingly. The wedding was five days off, and the British people were all-of- a-flutter at the thought of the pageantry and spectacle to come. He found that – as the big day grew ever closer – he was actually looking forward to it. He'd come to like Felicity very much. She was smart, funny, and fiercely opinionated – qualities he found extremely attractive in a future wife. He knew that she liked him. It worried him somewhat that she might more than like him, but he shrugged it off. He had no intention of going down *that* road and opening up any cans of worms.

He had a welcome day off. He was in the sky, at the controls of his five bladed H145 helicopter, and flying over Leith Hill Tower in the Surrey hills, drinking in the soul-cleansing scenery below, and unwinding from a hectic week spent delivering on his royal duties.

He'd tried to persuade Felicity to go flying with him. He thought she'd love the exhilaration of being at one with the sky, but she'd shaken her head emphatically and point-blank refused, so he was spending the day without her, and he missed her company.

He'd seen that she was afraid. It had surprised him. He never imagined that she could ever be afraid of anything, but helicopters seemed to be the exception. At first, he'd laughed, and then he'd seen the look of hurt in her eyes and realised she was serious.

It was a great pity. Flying was the greatest love of his life, and he was disappointed that he would never be able to share his passion with her.

Never say never, he thought – banking left and heading back towards London. He would work on her – get her to trust him as a pilot – and then get her in the air beside him.

He frowned, realising that he had absolutely no idea what her interests or hobbies were. He hadn't thought to ask. He recalled – all those years ago when they were a brief item – that she'd loved to write. He wondered if she still had dreams of being a published author. She hadn't mentioned it. He was determined to ask her about it as soon as he saw her again.

He scanned the audio panel on the cockpit. 'We're heading back,' he said into the radio on his helmet.

'Right,' his protection officer said from behind him.

'We'll go the scenic route.'

'Okay, boss.'

An hour later, he landed at the Barclay's Heliport, Battersea. His car was waiting. Glancing at his watch, he noted that he had three hours before he was due at Felicity's for dinner. He wasn't looking forward to it – not because he didn't want to see her, but because he didn't relish several hours in her mother's company.

The Lady Elizabeth Smythe-Walters wasn't his cup of tea. She was much too abrasive, exceptionally snobbish, and reminded him far too much of the women he'd grown up around. He thanked God that Felicity was nothing like her. There wasn't a snobbish bone in her body, and she would rather die than act the sycophant.

He was looking forward to meeting her father. He had flown over for the wedding, and that was the only reason he'd agreed to the dinner.

When he arrived back at the palace, he was still completely unaware of the trouble that was brewing quietly around him.

The first inclination that all was not well was when he was summoned by his mother. He tried to put her off, telling Horace that he was about to jump in the shower, but Horace had insisted.

Bemused, but not overly worried, he met with her in her private sitting room.

The first thing she said was, 'Why is your mobile phone switched off? I've been trying to get in touch with you for hours.'

His hand went automatically to the phone in his pocket. 'Sorry,' he said. 'I forgot to turn it back on. You know it's always off when I fly.'

'Yes, well, what if there was an emergency?'

'You can always have me reached by radio.'

'This isn't something I could put across the airwaves.'

'Oh?' He flopped down into a chair, still not worried.

'It's about Felicity.'

He was immediately alert. 'Has something happened to her?'

'You could say that.'

'Is she hurt?' He was back on his feet.

She flapped a hand. 'No, nothing like that. Sit back down. Looking up at you is giving me vertigo.'

He sat. 'What is it, then?'

'Earlier, the press office received a warning. There's a story expected to explode all over the media in a couple of hours.'

'About Felicity?' He suddenly realised what was about to happen. 'And her old boss... Robert Baker?'

The queen nodded and snorted down her long nose. 'It was bound to happen. You can't keep that sort of thing quiet.'

'Does she know?'

'Well, I certainly haven't told her.'

'I need to warn her.' He pushed himself back up off the chair once more.

'No, Louis. What you *must do* is prepare a statement.'

'Saying what?'

'Whatever you're advised to say by the press secretary.'

'I don't think...'

'No, that's perfectly true... you *don't* think. You insisted on having her, and – a few days before the wedding – her past comes back to haunt us all.'

'Her past is nobody's business, and *that's* what my statement will say.' He made for the door but was halted by her next words.

'You have to call it off. I don't care about the expense, or the uproar it will cause. There's no way you can marry her – not now.'

He turned slowly, steeling himself for the fury he knew was about to be hurled at him.

'I'm not calling it off,' he said. 'When you agreed that we could marry, you knew all about her past. You swallowed it because you were getting what you wanted. Well, mother – you'll have to go on swallowing it. I'm marrying her, and that's that.'

The expected fury didn't materialise. Instead, she looked at him with a cold detachment that froze him to the spot.

He cleared his throat and dropped his eyes. He couldn't bear to continue looking straight into the face of utter disdain.

He waited. It was her turn to speak.

'Very well,' she finally said. 'Have it your own way but be mindful of the fact that you will be playing right into the Prime Minister's hands. When he sees this evening's headlines, he'll be beside himself with glee.'

'I don't see why. I think the country will rally behind us. So, what if Felicity isn't perfect? The public will love her all the more for it, and they'll love me for standing by her.'

'He was a *married* man, Louis. No one will condone an affair with a married man.'

'You know that she denies it ever happened?'

She nodded. 'Who will believe her?'

Did he even believe her? Somehow, he thought that he did. In all the months they'd been engaged, he'd never raised the subject with her, but – the Felicity he now knew and respected – would never have had that affair. It simply wasn't who she was.

'How did the story break?'

'An anonymous source, I'm told.'

'What proof do they have?'

'You'll have to speak to the press secretary for that information.'

'Very well.' He gave her a curt nod and left her sitting staring after him.

Before he headed for the press office, he turned on his phone and called Felicity. He had to warn her and reassure her that everything was going to be all right.

'Hello, Louis?'

'Felicity?'

'Who else?'

He dragged in a breath. 'There's something I have to tell you... warn you about.'

'Oh?'

He heard the sudden unease in her voice, and wished he was by her side and not delivering the news over the phone. 'It's about Robert Baker.' A beat. 'The media have the story.'

She didn't immediately respond and, when she did, her words came out in one long sigh. 'There is no story,' she said. 'I never...'

'I know,' he put in, cutting her off. 'I know, Felicity.'

She was suddenly defensive. 'You know what?'

'That there is no story. I don't believe a single word of it.'

'You don't?' She was all choked-up. 'I thought... I thought...'

'I know you're not capable of such a thing... not an affair with someone already married.'

'I don't have any idea why he said that we did. It never made any sense.'

'Look,' he said hurriedly. 'I'm going to have a quick shower, and then I'm heading straight over, okay?'

'Okay.'

'We'll ride this out together. Nothing has changed. Do you understand?'

'Yes. Please hurry.'

Chapter Twenty-Three

S he ended the call and threw the phone down onto the table. It was frankly surreal. Amazingly, the fact that the story was about to break wasn't what shocked her most. What really amazed her was Louis saying that he believed her. They'd never spoken about it – not since way back – and she'd always understood that he'd simply accepted it as being true, and that he wasn't unduly perturbed.

She recalled how angry he'd been at his mother's dinner party. He'd certainly been perturbed about it then, but – afterwards – it was almost as if he'd wiped it from his mind.

She wished that she'd pursued the matter with Robert. There had to be a reason why he'd spouted such a lie, but she'd decided to let sleeping dogs lie.

Now those dogs had awakened, and she wasn't sure how much damage would now be done.

Louis must have broken every speed limit to reach her as quickly as he did. She hadn't mentioned anything to her parents, so they were surprised when he rolled up several hours too early for dinner and looking as if he'd just emerged from the shower.

He barrelled through the door, stood in the hallway, and found her with his eyes. Felicity raised an unsteady hand to her face and covered her mouth. She didn't want him to see her lips trembling. She wanted to appear strong and unmoved.

'Louis?' Her father stretched out a hand, and Louis grasped it absently. 'You're early.'

'Yes, sorry. Didn't Felicity say?'

'No, I didn't tell them,' she said in a voice almost too low to hear. 'I thought I'd wait until you got here.'

'What's going on?'

Felicity turned her eyes on her mother. 'We'd better go into the drawing room and sit down. We'll explain everything then.'

Her parents eyed one another, and then – by silent, mutual consent - they made their way across the hall to the room at the right of the stairs.

Felicity made to follow, but Louis stopped her with a hand on her arm. 'Wait a moment,' he said. 'Let's discuss what we're going to tell them.'

'My mother knows about Robert,' she returned.

He frowned. 'I thought...?'

'Only what was said when I was fired from my job. There was nothing else to tell her.'

'Does your father know?'

She nodded.

'Okay, then we'll simply explain what's about to happen.'

Her heart was in her mouth. 'Do you want to call the wedding off? I'd understand.'

'No,' he said. 'That's the last thing I want.'

'I wish...'

'What do you wish, Felicity?'

'That I'd been brave enough to take them all on at the time. I shouldn't have simply let it go. I lost my job over that stupid rumour... only, it wasn't a rumour, was it? Robert actually said that we... that we...' She shuddered. Even the thought of it made her feel dirty.

'I feel bad for believing him.'

'Why wouldn't you? I bet he was completely plausible.'

'He was, but it was his wife who convinced me.'

She fought the urge to simply bolt upstairs, lock herself in her room, and never come back out. She wasn't sure how she was going to face what was to come.

'What are we going to do?' she said. 'What does your mother want us to do?'

'Never mind my mother. It's up to us, and no one else.'

'Brave words, Louis, but it's going to feel as if the sky is crashing down on our heads.'

'I know.' He sounded almost defeated.

She had a sense that it was going to be harder on him than on her. He would be the one the media would go after.

'How do they know? I don't understand how they found out.'

'I didn't have time to ask the press secretary. I didn't waste any time getting here.'

'I don't think Robert would've repeated the lie to the press.'

'No, I agree. His wife would string him up if he aired that piece of dirty linen in public.'

'Who, then?' She thought a moment. 'Someone from the firm?'

He shrugged. 'Maybe.'

'Why leave it to so close to the wedding? It doesn't make any sense.'

'No, you're right. It almost feels like deliberate sabotage.'

He took her hand. 'Let's talk to your parents. This house is going to be under siege soon, and they need to be prepared.'

Her father stood in front of the huge stone fireplace, his hands behind his back, and his chin thrust forward. Her mother sat perched on the edge of the sofa. Their eyes were on them as soon as they stepped into the room.

'Well, Louis?' her father said. 'Care to tell us what's going on?'

He looked worried. Felicity always knew when her father was anxious. He had a particular way of rocking backwards and forwards on his heels whenever agitation lurked beneath his otherwise calm exterior. She felt heart-sorry for him. He'd come all the way from New York for a wedding and, instead, he was going to be met with a circus.

Her mother plucked at the neck of her dress, showing that – she too – was anxious.

'I'm not going to beat about the bush,' Louis said. 'That ridiculous story about Felicity and her boss is about to go viral. My mother had advance warning, but we've probably only got about another hour before it hits social media. Thereafter, the news vans will be parked outside your front door.'

'Oh, is that all?'

Felicity looked at her father with a shocked expression. She saw him steady, and then cease rocking. He looked extremely relieved.

'Don't you understand, dad?' she said. 'That lie is going to cause a whole heap of trouble.'

'Lies always do,' he returned. 'But liars never prosper. Whoever fed the media that false information is going to live to regret it.' He sighed. 'For a moment, I thought you were going to tell me that someone was dying... or dead. I'm just relieved that it's something as mundane as a scandalous lie.'

'The liar might not prosper,' Louis put in. 'In fact, I'm sure that whoever it is will end up falling flat on their face, but the damage will have been done by then.'

'Not if we get in first.'

'What do you mean?'

'You say we have an hour?'

Louis nodded. 'About that, I guess.'

'Then, let's use it. I suggest we get straight round to this Robert chap's house, confront him, and force him to retract.'

'I don't think it was Robert who spoke to the press, dad,' Felicity said.

'You might be right, but – if you both deny the affair – the media will be left with a damp squib.'

'I know where he lives,' Louis said, warming to her father's idea. 'It'll take us less than twenty minutes to get there.'

'Okay, what are we waiting for?' He made for the door. 'Just let me grab my jacket.'

'Are you sure this is a good idea?' Felicity said to Louis. 'It could backfire terribly.'

'I can't think of anything else to pour cold water on this,' he replied, squeezing her hand reassuringly.

'Then, I'm coming with you,' she said. 'I want to look him in the eye and hear him take it all back.'

He looked ready to refuse but thought better of it when he saw the steely determination in her eyes.

'Okay but let me do the talking.'

She nodded. 'Deal.'

Chapter Twenty-Four

They didn't get there in time. Fate conspired against them and placed a serious collision of several cars in their path.

By the time they rolled into Robert's Street, the press was already there.

Felicity forced herself not to panic. The story had broken, and a low, desperate moan escaped her lips. Louis put his arm around her and hugged her close. Her father, in the front seat with the driver, peered out the window and cursed under his breath. The atmosphere in the car was now fraught with tension.

The car rolled to a stop at the junction at the head of the street. The driver looked over his shoulder and asked Louis what he should do.

'They haven't spotted us,' he said. 'Let's just get out of here.'

Louis' phone chirruped in his pocket. He took one look at the screen and scowled. It was his mother. He turned it off.

It was time to consider a plan B.

'Take it head-on,' her father advised. 'No hiding, no waiting, no flummery. Get right up in their faces.'

'It's not that simple,' Louis returned. 'I'll have to take advice from the press office.' He slumped down in his seat but kept a tight hold on Felicity. 'They'll want to draft a statement.'

'A bland denial?' He shook his head. 'That won't work.'

'There's no point in stoking the fire, George. The least said, the better.'

'I don't agree. You both have to show the world how furious you are at this lie.'

'That's not how it's done.'

'Well, do it differently, this time. Get the public on your side from the get-go. The story hasn't taken wings, so now is the time to strike... when the press is least expecting it.'

'It would be more than my life was worth to break protocol.'

'This is my daughter's reputation we're talking about.'

Felicity was shocked by her father's rare burst of emotion. 'Calm down, dad. Louis will do what's right.'

'For *him*, maybe.'

'For Felicity, too,' Louis snapped, suddenly angry. 'I know what I have to do.'

He'd already formulated a plan, and his mother wasn't going to like it.

'Does it involve standing up for my daughter... showing everyone that you back her side of the story one hundred per cent?'

'Of course, it does, but I'm not going to turn this into any more of a circus than it already is. A cool head... and mouth... is what's required.' He turned his phone back on, brought up a number, and waited as it rang out.

Glad that the verbal ping-pong match between her father and Louis was over – for the moment, at least – Felicity relaxed a little and listened to the one-sided conversation Louis was having on the phone with the royal press secretary.

When he'd finished, he turned to her and said, 'Ring your mother, and tell her to get a taxi to the palace... we'll meet her there. Tell her to leave immediately, before her street is jammed with reporters.'

Thankfully, the remainder of the journey was made in silence. Once at Buckingham Palace, they sat in the car until Felicity's mother arrived, and all four entered together.

It was obvious that the queen was more than a little upset at the arrival of the impromptu guests. She threw her son a look of utter disdain and invited everyone to sit.

Momentarily, they were joined in the sitting room by Louis' father, Horace, and the press secretary.

Louis didn't beat about the bush. When everyone was settled, he stood, and said, 'Before we get down to business, I want to get one thing clear.'

Everyone sat to attention. His serious tone, and the determined expression on his face, that brooked no argument, even had the queen taking particular notice of what he had to say.

'Felicity *did not* have an affair with that man... this Robert Baker. As I see it, she's been slandered and – now that we are about to see that defamation in print – she is about to suffer from libel. I won't allow that to go unpunished.' He turned to his mother. 'I realise this isn't the way we do things around here, but Felicity is just about to become a member of the royal family, and I won't stand by and watch as she's torn to shreds over something she didn't do, so...' He dragged in a breath. 'I want legal proceedings to commence immediately. I want the full might of your legal team behind this, mother.'

The queen paled. She opened her mouth to deny him, but a small shake of her husband's head stalled her. She didn't often pay heed to her feckless husband's wishes, but she saw the pleading in his eyes, and held back on her refusal. She wanted to hear what he had to say on the matter. She turned to fully face him, her eyes asking the question.

'I agree with Louis,' he said, then, standing and stretching his neck, added, 'There's been more than one story about me in the tabloids that have been out and out lies. According to most headlines, I've slept my way across the whole country, and beyond. That's simply not true.' He gave his wife an apologetic smile. 'I'm not quite the rogue I've been painted.'

The queen's lips thinned, and her eyes narrowed, but she allowed him to continue.

'I often wished that I could've swept the lot of them into court, but I knew that wasn't what you wanted, my dear, so I suffered the lies in silence. I don't want Louis and Felicity to begin their married life under the strain of knowing their every move will be twisted and falsely reported. We need to put a stop to it now.'

'That would be a mistake,' Horace piped in, his attention fully on the queen. 'It will send the wrong message. It will look as if the monarchy is using its influence to silence the press on the unsavoury exploits of some members of the family. The public will believe you are using your power and money to stifle free speech.'

'That's utter rubbish, Horace,' Louis snapped. 'And, who asked for your opinion, anyway? You always have far too much to say.'

'I value his opinion,' the queen said forcefully. 'Everyone in this room will speak in strictest confidence, and everyone will be given their say.' She turned to her friend. 'What do you think, Elizabeth.' There seemed to be a warning note in the queen's voice. It was obvious what she wanted her to say.

Felicity's mother seemed to shrink into the cushions of the sofa. She didn't want to voice an opinion on the matter. She wanted to leave the decision wholly at the queen's feet. Whatever she decided would be fine with her, but, as she glanced at her daughter's teary-eyed face, she felt sudden shame. She was aware of her husband at her side and, when he took her hand and squeezed it reassuringly, she found the strength to – for the first time in her life – put someone else first.

'I won't have my daughter maligned,' she said. Felicity gasped, and that gasp further shamed her, because it was obvious that her daughter was shocked to hear those words escape her mouth. 'I agree with Louis... legal action has to be taken.'

Although it wasn't what the queen wanted to hear, for the moment, she let it go. It would be enough that Elizabeth would no longer be welcome within her select circle of friends.

'It goes without saying that I agree with Louis.' That was Felicity's father. 'And I think – before the hour is out – a statement from the family's most senior solicitor should be personally read out in front of the cameras.'

'That's not all,' Louis said. 'I want the source named.'

'The press never reveals their sources,' Horace said.

'They will, this time. I don't believe that a person spouting a lie, and defaming an innocent person, will be protected by the courts. That goes for Robert Baker as well.' He dropped his eyes to Felicity. 'If you want, we'll also sue your previous employers for unfair dismissal.'

She nodded. It was what she wanted.

He smiled and gave a curt nod. To everyone in the room, he added, 'The wedding will go ahead, as planned. We have a short window of time to get the ball rolling on the legal stuff. I agree with George – we need that statement read out within the hour.'

Apart from Horace, the queen stood alone. Ultimately, it didn't matter what the others thought. The decision was hers to make. She wavered. It was a pivotal moment, and one that would change the face of the monarchy forever. Either way, considerable damage would be done. She wondered what way would present as the lesser of the two evils.

'Please, mother.' Louis hunkered down at her knees and took hold of her hands. 'Stand by me in this.'

'Your majesty...' Horace interjected. 'This would be highly irregular and foolish.'

She nodded, and no one in the room knew what the nod represented. Was it in agreement with her son, or with Horace?

'Mother?' Louis stared directly into her eyes. 'Do you stand with me?'

She gave a second nod and everyone, with the exception of her private secretary, breathed a sigh of relief.

It was agreed.

Chapter Twenty-Five

Her heart crashed. Her whole world tipped precariously on its axis. The sea of faces, the cameras, the loud, incessant questions being fired at her from all directions, in every language imaginable, completely stunned her. She'd thought – rather naively – that the statement from the queen's personal solicitor would have been the end of it. She had no idea that it would only be the beginning.

She was alone, emerging from her house to drive to lunch with Alice, when she was met with a wall of people all baying and screaming at her. She had no well-honed instincts to fall back on. Nothing like that had ever happened to her before, and she had no idea what to do. She took a step towards them – meaning to push her way through to her car – but it had the effect of creating a huge surge of bodies towards her.

The myriad of voices morphed into one huge block of sound. The pushing and the jostling almost took her off her feet. She was terrified, numb, and completely overwhelmed.

And, then she was rescued.

When his arms went around her, and when she caught the scent of the familiar cologne, she went limp with relief.

Louis had arrived to save her.

Three of his protection officers circled, effectively shielding them from the sea of reporters. They created enough space to enable him to lift her into his arms and carry her back inside the house.

'I'm so sorry,' he said, over and over again, hugging her and stroking her hair. 'I should've known. I'm so sorry.'

He'd been warned not to speak to them. The matter was in the hands of the solicitors. He had to take no action, make no statement, and keep out of the limelight. It was the price he agreed to pay in order to get his mother's support with the legal action.

'I thought...'

'I know... I know. It's all got out of hand. I have to do something.'

Felicity pulled back and groped for a chair. She was finding it difficult to fully comprehend what was happening. Some of the questions that had been fired at her – those few that blasted past her confusion and reached her ears – had shocked her. They were personal questions, accusatory questions. In spite of the very clear statement issued only the night before, she'd been branded a harlot.

'What can you do, Louis? They've ignored everything that's been said.'

'Well, I haven't said anything, have I?' He made for the door, and she reached out and grabbed his arm.

'Wait, please. Don't leave me.' She hated feeling so vulnerable. She hated herself for being too weak to stand up for herself. This wasn't her. She wasn't a victim. 'If you're going back out there, then so am I.'

'What?' He turned and looked down at her in horror. 'You can't go out there. They'll eat you alive.'

'Then, neither are you. I'm sick of everyone else talking for me. I haven't been allowed to answer a single question. I've been effectively gagged by my parents, your parents... even by *you*, Louis.'

He sighed with frustration. 'Let me deal with it.'

'No.'

'It's for your own good.'

'How dare you.' The words were uttered quietly. Nevertheless, they resonated. 'How dare you say that to me.' She stood. Her legs no longer felt like rubber. Her heart pounded. 'What do you see, when you look at me, Louis? Do you see someone who's incapable of speaking up for herself?'

'I see someone who is out of her depth, Felicity. That mob out there are out for your blood. You have to leave it to me.'

And there it was – the one statement that, if she let it slide, would effectively set the scene for their whole life together. *Leave it to me.*

As if she would.

'You know what, Louis? I'm not going to leave it to you, and – better still – you can stay in the house. I don't need you holding my hand, and I certainly don't need you to speak for me.'

He wanted to argue the point with her. He wanted to protect her, but she clearly wasn't going to allow him to, so he shrugged and stepped to the side.

'They're all yours,' he said. 'Give me a shout if you need any help.'

She wasn't afraid – or, at least that's what she told herself as she stepped back out through the door.

The noise was deafening and extremely disorienting. She wondered how anyone expected her to understand anything of what was being screamed at her.

Louis was directly behind her and, although she'd wanted him to stay in the house, she excused him his proximity. As long as he kept his mouth shut, she'd forgive him hovering over her.

At the sight of her, the noise intensified. No one dared to actually step onto the property, and the three protection officers did a good job of keeping them from surging forward any further than the kerb.

Felicity remained silent. She refused to attempt to speak over the noise. If they wanted to hear what she had to say, they would have to quieten down and become more orderly.

At first, they kept trying to goad her into responding to their questions. When that failed, they threw statements at her that were enough to make her blush. She felt Louis step forward when her morals were called into question, but she held a handout to the side and gestured for him to remain where he was.

One by one, the reporters understood the situation and the noise began to abate. A full ten minutes passed – with Felicity simply standing on the step staring down at them – before complete silence reigned.

She was acutely aware of every face, every camera, and every micro-phone. She breathed in their scent of sweat. She felt the cool afternoon breeze on her skin. She felt calm.

'I have a short statement to make,' she said, and staggered back a step when her voice acted as the catalyst for everyone to begin shouting again all at once.

Stupid people.

She dragged in a breath and returned to silent mode.

They were finally getting it. If they spoke, she would go quiet. If they remained quiet, she would speak.

She tried again.

'I want to make a short statement. I haven't prepared anything. I don't have anything written down, so please understand that this is an impromptu few words.' She cleared her throat, straightened her spine, and threw her chin up. She was determined that they were going to see a strong person speak – someone who was sure of herself, and sure of what she was about to say. She was mindful of how her words could be edited and twisted, so she determined to keep her speech short and to the point.

'I don't know any of you,' she went on. 'I haven't had the privilege of speaking to the press before now, so forgive the fact that I don't know any of your names.' She swept her eyes across the crowd, resting on one or two faces for a second or more.

'I don't know any of you, but you obviously believe that you know me.' She forced a smile and ensured that it reached her eyes. ''I'm not going to argue with your opinion of me. You're entitled to it, but I ask that you reserve judgement until all the facts are known. There are sev-eral legal cases pending. I believe that you already know the details of those, so I won't bore you with repeating them. Suffice to say...' She cleared her throat for a second time.

Full honesty, Felicity.

'I've loved Louis... the Prince of Wales... since I was eighteen years old. Marrying him is a dream come true. I can't wait to walk up the aisle and see him waiting for me. He's handsome, isn't he ladies?' She rested her eyes on one female reporter after another and was gratified to see them nod and smile. 'I'm a lucky woman – I know I am.'

Here goes.

'And I've saved myself for him.'

The collective gasp was so loud that no one heard her final words. Everyone stared at her with open mouths and expressions of extreme shock. No one could quite believe what they'd just heard. She had – in front of several television cameras – admitted to being a virgin. Who did that? And better still - who believed her?

What was the queen going to say?

'What is the queen going to say?' Louis asked, when they were safely back inside. 'You've just lied to the world's press, Felicity, and she's going to go ballistic.'

'Who said I lied?'

'You didn't lie?' He almost choked on the words.

'Well, I said that I'd saved myself for you... that was a little white lie.'

'It's a *huge* lie. You can't make out that you're a virgin, for goodness' sake. Quite apart from it being an untrue statement, it isn't something to be shared with a bunch of reporters.'

'That's not the part that's the lie.' She blushed despite her effort not to. 'I should've said that I saved myself for the man I was going to marry, not specifically for you, but technically - as I *am* marrying you – it wasn't even a lie at all.'

She scurried through to the kitchen before he had a chance to respond to that little nugget of information.

He was slow to follow her. He was finding it difficult to get his head around her news.

A virgin? He couldn't quite believe it. She was twenty-eight years old, beautiful, desirable, and passionate. *How was that even possible*?

He hoped there was wine in the fridge. He desperately needed an alcohol hit.

He found her washing up at the sink. Her back was to him, and he was glad that he didn't have to look at her just yet. He was embarrassed, and he was shocked, but what he really felt was fear.

He was about to marry a virgin, and the responsibility of that was terrifying.

She heard him rummaging about in the fridge. She knew that he was looking for wine. She was desperate for a glass or two herself, and she dried her hands and went to help in locating a bottle.

'We only have red,' she said. 'Merlot. You'll find a few bottles in the wine rack by the back door.

He nodded, avoiding her eyes. He wasn't ready to look at her.

'Corkscrew?' He waved the bottle in front of her face.

She opened the cutlery drawer and handed it to him.

She stared at the top of his head as he bent over the bottle. He was taking it badly, she thought. He was probably disappointed.

'Are you disappointed, Louis?'

He threw his head up, 'Disappointed?'

'That I'm a virgin?'

'Why would that disappoint me?'

'I know nothing about sex... well, nothing other than what I've been told, or what I've read, or what I've seen on TV. I imagine you'd want your future wife to be experienced.'

'Don't talk such utter rot, Felicity.'

'You don't want an experienced wife?'

'I just want you.' He meant it. Virgin, or not, he still wanted her to be his wife.

'Because I know all the family secrets, and because I'm willing to endure a loveless marriage without complaint?'

'Something along those lines, yes.' He popped the cork and opened a few cupboards looking for glasses. He found them and set two on the table.

'You said you'd loved me since you were eighteen years old,' he reminded her. 'The marriage won't be completely loveless, then, will it?'

'That's just as well,' she returned, accepting a glass filled to the brim with wine. 'You want children, I presume?'

'Of course.'

'We both grew up with parents who couldn't stand the sight of one another. I won't wish that on our children. One-sided love is still love, and our children will grow up knowing there's love between us... even if it only comes from me.'

He stared at her over the rim of his glass. 'I wouldn't have asked you to marry me if I'd known.'

'That I'm a virgin, or that I'm still in love with you?'

'Both.'

'Do you want to call the whole thing off?'

'After what you've just announced to the world? Are you mad?'

She smirked. 'Not so you'd notice. I don't think we'll be hearing much more about Robert Baker. My virginity will be the sole news topic for weeks.'

'My mother still won't be pleased.'

'She'll get over it.'

'I still can't believe you made that announcement... that you'd saved yourself for me. It kinda scares me.'

'It's making you feel guilty?'

'You could say that.'

'It shouldn't change anything.'

'Are you joking? I already thought I was ruining your life.'

She sipped her wine. She understood where he was coming from. He probably believed that he now had an obligation to at least try to be faithful to her as payment for her sacrifice – a sacrifice he now knew to be much greater than he originally thought.

'I'm not asking anything of you,' she said.

'Well, you should. You have a right to be loved back, Felicity. You have a right to a happy future with a man who returns your feelings.'

'I'm happy to settle for you. I know what I've agreed to, and I don't regret finally accepting your proposal.'

'If you're hoping...'

She held up her hand. 'I have no hopes beyond being your wife.'

He smiled. 'Let's get drunk. My mother can be better tolerated when one is sozzled.'

'I'd be happy to get drunk with you, Louis.'

He tipped his glass at her. 'You're one special lady, Felicity.'

'And don't you forget it.'

Chapter Twenty-Six

'Are you drunk yet?'

'Not quite.' Felicity tipped the last of the wine from the bottle into her glass and then flopped down onto the sofa next to Louis. 'I'm getting there, though.'

'Me, too.'

They were both relaxed and rather mellow. Neither allowed their thoughts to dwell on the consequences of her impromptu address to the media, and both ignored the fact that they would soon have a reckoning with the queen over what was said. They were content to sit quietly, sip their wine, and talk of nothing in particular.

The wine loosened their tongues, and no silly topic of conversation was avoided.

Louis regaled her with stories of his last year at university, and she giggled in all the right places, and countered with stories of her own that made him throw his head back and roar with laughter.

They were having fun. They sparked off one another. Louis became more and more convinced about how compatible they were, and Felicity simply savoured the private, intimate time with him. She began to imagine that their future together would mean that every evening with him would be as perfect.

She rested her head on his shoulder. The weight of her head unnerved him. The scent of her perfume was intoxicating. The atmosphere shifted.

After a long silence, Louis said, 'You didn't mean it, did you?'

She felt a flutter of alarm. His voice suddenly sounded very sober. 'Mean what?'

'About being in love with me?'

'You know I meant it, Louis.'

'That's what I thought.'

She lifted her head to look at him. 'I wouldn't let it worry you. It's my problem.'

'It does, though... worry me.'

'Well, it shouldn't.'

The evening was quickly becoming soured. It suddenly wasn't fun anymore.

He clenched his jaw. There were things he wanted to say – ought to say – but he feared where they would lead.

'I think I'd better go,' he said, pushing himself to his feet. 'I've got a great deal of explaining to do.'

'Do you want me to come with you? I'm the one your mother should have a go at.'

He shook his head. 'Best leave that for another day.'

'I'm not afraid of her.'

He smiled. 'Not many people can say that.'

'Her bark is worse than her bite.'

'True, but you've not really witnessed how nasty that bark can be.'

'I'm not sorry, Louis.'

'I know.'

'I won't apologise for speaking the truth.'

'No one is going to ask that of you.'

He stepped back from the sofa, distancing himself from her. She sat there, looking up at him, and her expression unnerved him. He wished he knew what she wanted from him. He was sure that it was much more than he could give.

'Tell the queen that I'll refrain from speaking to the press again. Reassure her that it was a one-off.'

He nodded and grabbed his jacket from the back of the chair. 'I will, and I'm sure it will go some way towards knocking the edge off her tongue.'

'When will I see you again?'

He thought he detected a plaintive note in her voice. He closed his eyes briefly. He wanted to say *never*. He wanted to walk out and not have to deal with a virgin bride, and especially not one that loved him. It wasn't what he'd signed up for.

The problem was that he really liked her. He didn't want to hurt her but had the sense to know that hurting her was inevitable.

'Not for a few days,' he said. 'I have to go to Edinburgh tomorrow.'

'Can I come with you?'

He shook his head. 'That wouldn't be a good idea.'

'Why not?'

'It just wouldn't, okay?' He forced his arms into his jacket, nearly tearing the lining in the process. He was suddenly angry. – at himself, more than her. He'd been an utter fool, and they were both going to pay for his foolishness by a lifetime of misery.

She stood. She reached up on her tiptoes and her breath fanned across his face. He stepped back and she grabbed his arms.

'Don't leave... not like this.'

'Like what?'

'All het-up and mad as hell.' She reached up and stroked his cheek. 'It's going to be okay,' she said. 'I promise.'

'I wish that I could believe that.'

'It's too late for second thoughts.'

He knew that. Her words to the media had all but made it impossible for him to jilt her weeks before the wedding. The whole country would now know that she was in love with him – had always been in love with him. Any doubts anyone had about the validity of their upcoming union, would've been smashed to smithereens, and - if he walked away now - he would be vilified.

He dragged in a breath. 'I'm not having second thoughts.'

'Liar.' She smiled to lessen the sting of the accusation. 'You want to run as far away from this wedding as you can.'

'That's not going to happen.'

'I know.'

She reached up and pressed her lips lightly against his mouth. He was taken completely by surprise. His reaction wasn't exactly flattering. He jumped back, as if electrocuted.

He met her gaze. He saw fire in her eyes, and something else – hunger.

The muscles in his jaw were so tense that his whole face hurt. It took a tremendous effort not to grab her and crush her mouth with his, to press himself against her and show her how much he wanted her. The invitation was right there in her eyes, and he was tempted – so very tempted – but wanting her was a curse, and not something it was safe to succumb to.

'I'm sorry,' he said. 'I have to go.'

She stood, her arms now hanging limply at her sides, and watched as he turned from her and walked away. There was a slump to his shoulders that spoke volumes. His tread was weary. He didn't hurry from the room, and she hoped that he'd turn back to her.

He didn't.

She wasn't sure how long she stood there after he'd gone. By the time she dropped back down onto the sofa her legs were numb.

That was stupid.

She rocked forward onto her elbows and nodded silently to herself. She felt excruciatingly embarrassed, and hurt, and disappointed – but, mostly embarrassed.

What had she been thinking? What if he'd taken her up on her silent offer?

She groaned and dropped her head into her hands. He'd turned her down. She'd all but thrown herself at him, and he'd walked away.

The rejection stung far more than the relief.

She rubbed her stinging eyes. She wanted to cry, but the tears seemed to be under caution not to spring free from behind her lids.

Her phone trilled. She ignored it. Someone knocked at the front door, then hammered on it. Louis' protection detail had obviously left with him, leaving her vulnerable to prying reporters.

The hammering became an incessant irritant, and she jumped to her feet and stomped out to the hallway and screamed at, whoever it was, to get lost.

'Felicity... open up.'

It was Alice.

She almost collapsed with relief and dragged open the door. Alice stumbled across the threshold, three reporters literally pushing at her back.

'It's a circus out there,' she huffed. 'I tried ringing you. Why aren't you picking up?'

Felicity gave her an *are you kidding me* look.

'Oh, right... the reporters. I guess they've been calling you constantly?'

'No, not really, but I wasn't about to take any chances.'

'Duh! You would've seen it was me, silly.'

'What are you doing here?'

'Louis rang me... asked me to pop over.'

Great... not!

'I'd rather be on my own.'

'He said you'd say that.'

'What else did he say?'

She shrugged. 'Nothing much.' She grinned. 'I saw you on the news. What possessed you to tell the world that you're a virgin?'

'It felt like a good idea at the time.' She led the way back through to the drawing room. 'I wish I'd kept my mouth shut, but all that rubbish about me and Robert was getting out of hand. I had to say *something.*'

'And, what about sharing the news that you've always loved Louis? I didn't know that. You never told me that.'

'It wasn't something I wanted to share with anyone.'

'Well, I guessed. You're not brilliant at hiding your feelings.'

The tears finally came. They spurted from her eyes in an explosion of angst, and she threw herself, into her friend's arms.

'Oh, Alice,' she sobbed. 'I think I need to call the whole thing off. I repulse him. I want him so much, but ... but he made it perfectly clear he's not interested.'

'That can't be true.'

'He... he rejected me,' she wailed. 'He doesn't want me.'

Chapter Twenty-Seven

She met Charles and Ronald, her newly appointed protection officers, the next morning. No one had told her to expect them and, at first, she'd refused them entry to the house.

They showed her their credentials. They were deployed from SO14 – a special branch of the London Metropolitan Police Force – and, although everything seemed perfectly in order, she still wouldn't allow them over the doorstep until she'd confirmed their authenticity with Louis.

She swallowed back hard when she noticed the fourteen missed calls, the fourteen voicemail messages, and the eight text messages – all from Louis.

How drunk had she been? She'd slept through an avalanche of attempts to contact her.

'I told him you were all right,' her mother said, walking into the kitchen and pouring herself a cup of coffee. 'He rang me, worried sick and wondering if you'd been abducted, and I told him you were out cold and drunk as a skunk.'

'When was that?'

'Oh, about four this morning. Apparently, he'd been ringing and texting you from around midnight.'

'Why didn't he come and check for himself?'

'He's on his way to Edinburgh. Didn't he mention that to you?'

She searched her memory, and vaguely recalled something about Edinburgh. She nodded, and gratefully accepted the cup of coffee her mother handed her. 'I drank a little too much wine,' she said.

She raised a perfectly plucked eyebrow. 'I noticed.'

'I was upset,' she said, defensively.

'There are more than you upset, Felicity. The queen, for one.'

'You've spoken to her?'

'A more accurate description would be – *she* spoke to *me*.'

She groaned and steadied herself with a hand on the granite work-top. 'Louis was going to explain everything to her.'

'She wasn't interested in what Louis had to say. It's you she wants to hear an explanation from.'

'Does she want me to go and see her?'

'Yes, but she's busy most of today. She expects you at the palace first thing tomorrow morning.'

'I have a dress fitting then.'

'You'll have to rearrange it.'

'I'm not going to apologise to her for what I said to those reporters.' Her defiance was a little weary, and – even to her own ears – she didn't sound convincing.

'That's up to you. I wouldn't dream of advising you on the matter.'

Her jaw dropped open. *Where had her real mother gone?*

'You needn't look at me like that, Felicity. Your father and I have decided to keep well out of this debacle.'

'You... and daddy? Since when have either of you ever agreed on anything?'

'Some things transcend the usual hostilities. This is one of those things.'

She sighed and sipped her coffee. If both of her parents were in agreement to keep well away from the flack, it must be really bad. She picked up the remote for the small television hanging on the kitchen wall and turned it on to a news channel.

'I wouldn't,' her mother said. 'It'll only upset you.' She reached over and plucked the remote from her hand. The television blacked out.

'Go and let those two nice men in. I'll make them a coffee whilst you have a shower.'

She'd completely forgotten about the two officers left standing on the doorstep. 'Do you know who they are?'

'Of course. Louis...'

'Told you?'

'Yes. He would've told you – if you'd picked up. One, or other, of them is going to be with you twenty-four-seven.'

'Brilliant.'

They came with a car – a Jaguar XJ – and that car was the only part of the arrangement she knew she was going to like. When she allowed them in, she saw it sitting shiny and sleek at the kerbside. The view was spoiled by the news van and the huddle of reporters milling around on the road. When they saw her, they moved forward, but she had the door closed before they'd taken more than a few steps.

She left the officers with her mother and plodded back upstairs.

She didn't feel well. She'd sat up with Alice most of the night – drinking wine and eating pizza – and the morning after that rather punishing night before had brought a brutal headache and painful memories.

She should've heard her phone ringing or buzzing with messages. It had been by her side, within arm's reach, the whole night. When she picked it up and checked it, she wasn't surprised to see that she'd put it on silent mode.

She couldn't make herself feel sorry that she'd caused Louis to worry about her.

She felt a flush of shame. She was becoming mightily fed up with feeling that way about herself. Ever since Louis had barged his way back into her life, she'd been ashamed about how she felt about him, ashamed about wanting him, ashamed about agreeing to marry him, ashamed about confiding her feelings to all and sundry, ashamed for making a pass at him and now, ashamed for stupidly muting her phone.

That was far too much shame.

If she actually had any sense, she would walk away. She would ask her father to take her back to New York with him and try to forget all about Louis. She'd leave one hell of a mess behind, and it was likely that her action would put the final nail in the monarchy's coffin, but – for her sake – it was probably the best thing to do.

She seriously considered it – for all of five seconds.

Who was she trying to kid? She'd never leave him.

Before stepping into the shower, she wrapped a towel around her body and brought up Louis' private number on her phone. She needed to hear his voice, and she needed to reassure him that he had no need to worry about her.

The call went to voicemail. She thought about leaving a message but decided against it. She'd try him again later.

The shower revived her somewhat, and she decided to try and move the next day's dress fitting to that afternoon. The local designer was working predominantly on her wedding gown and should be able to accommodate the change of arrangement.

Marcie Potter was a young, up and coming designer. Felicity chose her because she loved her repertoire, but also because she was in a position to get the dress designed, finished, and perfectly fitted before the big day – an enormous feat considering the short engagement and imminent ceremony.

She was in luck – Marcie was only too pleased to reschedule.

Felicity wanted her mother to accompany her. She'd never seen her in the dress and hadn't been privy to its design. Her mother was too busy, so – disappointed – she went, accompanied by both protection officers.

It wasn't the way it was supposed to be. Nothing was. She shook her disappointment off. There was no point in pining for what would never be.

Of course, the paparazzi followed the car.

Her phoned pinged and she automatically reached for it, hoping it was a message from Louis.

It wasn't. It was a news notification. It reminded her that Alice had set the notifications up on her phone the night before, saying, *you'd best keep an eye on what's being said... be prepared, girl.*

She smiled when she thought of how Alice seemed to have morphed into a mother hen. All night, she'd poured wine down her throat, sympathised, commiserated, and generally rallied behind her. She'd promised to be her friend forever – no matter what. It didn't matter that she was completely sozzled when she'd said it. Felicity had recognised the genuine truth in her words.

She swiped the screen and opened the headline.

Virgin fiancé waits at home as playboy prince meets up with old flame.

There was a photograph. She blinked and then focussed.

Louis was standing with a hand on the arm of some woman, leaning in and smiling, and Felicity felt a jolt of shock.

Her eyes dropped to the caption beneath the photograph.

The Prince of Wales arrived in Edinburgh, and straight into the arms of Fiona McBride – one time lover, and heiress to the Lasso Brewery empire.

She closed her eyes and dragged in a breath. She told herself it was nothing. Louis wasn't that stupid, and he certainly knew not to be indiscreet. There was, most likely, a perfectly good reason for the meeting.

Nevertheless, she felt as if she'd been punched in the gut. She'd wanted to go to Edinburgh with him. She couldn't think of a reason as to why he'd refused. Now, she thought she knew the reason.

Fiona McBride.

The more she stared at the picture, and the more she took in the smile in his eyes, the tender clutch at Fiona's arm, the more she came to realise that he didn't care about being discreet. She'd admitted to loving him, and that photograph, and that headline, was his response. It was a warning, a heads-up. He was showing her how it was going to be.

She suffered through the dress fitting. She didn't muster a tear or a smile when she saw how beautiful she looked in the mirror. She was alone on a day that should've been one of the happiest of her life. She couldn't help but think that it was a sign of things to come.

Before the car pulled up outside her mother's house, she had her phone out. She spoke to Horace, cancelling the meeting with the queen in the morning and apologising for the inconvenience. She refused to give an explanation, except to say that something more important had come up.

Once inside the house, she ran upstairs and packed a suitcase.

She was going to Edinburgh.

Chapter Twenty-Eight

'I'm sorry, but it's impossible,' Ronald said.

He was the smaller of the two bodyguards, and the one that Felicity liked the least. There was nothing wrong with him. He was a pleasant enough man, and he wasn't objectionable in any way, but he simply annoyed her. It was the way he looked at her – as if he pitied her.

'I'll take my own car, then,' she replied irritably. 'You can stay here and explain to everyone why you allowed me to drive all the way to Scotland on my own.'

'It's just not protocol,' he returned, attempting to keep his impatience at bay. 'We'd have to plan ahead... look at contingencies should there be an accident on the motorway, or...'

'I'm not listening to this. I'm not married into this protocol nonsense yet, so I can do what I want, when I want.'

'Does the prince know you're going?'

'No, and I have no plans to tell him. It's a surprise.'

She saw the knowing look pass over his eyes. He'd obviously seen the headline. She flushed. More shame.

'You *do* know how this will look,' her mother put in. 'You'll look like a fool, chasing after him.'

'I'm not chasing after him, and everyone can think what they like.'

'On your own head be it, then.'

Her father entered the fray. He said, 'Think about this, Felicity. This is no more than a knee-jerk reaction to a stupid photograph.'

'It's got nothing to do with the photograph,' she lied, and then said, 'Okay – it has *everything* to do with the photograph. I have to see him... find out what's going on.'

'Ring him,' her mother said. 'Let him explain.'

'I rang him this morning – before that awful headline – and he hasn't replied. I'm not phoning him again.' She turned back to Ronald. 'So, what's it to be?'

He sighed. 'I'll clear it, and we can be on our way in ten minutes.' He turned to his colleague. 'You up for it?'

Charles nodded. 'If it's what the lady wants.'

The car journey took seven hours. They stopped briefly twice and arrived just short of midnight.

Felicity wasn't sure if someone had surreptitiously warned Louis that she was on her way. She had no idea what to expect when she rolled up to Holyrood House, the official royal residence. She knew that she could either walk in and find him in an uncompromising situation with Fiona, or she could find him waiting on her with innocence stamped across his face.

Either way, she realised it wasn't going to be pretty. He would be furious.

She didn't look her best. Her hair hung like rat's tails over her shoulder, and her face was blotchy. Her clothes were wrinkled, and she was in desperate need of a shower. She knew the impression her appearance would give, and she didn't care. Let the next morning's photograph show her arriving looking much the worse for wear. Let the world witness her determination to have her man.

Standing at the end of Edinburgh's Royal Mile, the palace of Holyrood House was an imposing fixture.

They drove through the gate and entered the castle yard. They had to sit in the car for a full fifteen minutes before they were granted permission to enter.

Louis was waiting. He stood alone at the bottom of the Great Stairs. He dismissed Charles and Ronald with a curt nod of his head, and then turned his full attention on her.

She almost wilted beneath his gaze. She tried to read him, but his eyes were hooded, and his features set.

'Surprise,' she croaked.

He remained silent, and she was forced to walk towards him. She wondered if he was angry because she'd spoiled his plans for the night.

'I'm not sorry,' she said. It wasn't lost on her the fact that she'd uttered that statement more than once those past few days.

'When are you ever sorry, Felicity?'

She was grateful for his words. At least he was speaking to her. That, at least, was something.

'You've caused mayhem back home. My mother was all for sending the police after you.'

'You knew I was coming, then?'

'Of course, I knew.'

'You didn't ring me... try to stop me.'

'Would there have been a point to that?'

She shook her head.

'I thought not.'

'Are you very angry with me?'

He thought about that, then refrained from answering.

'Is Fiona here?' She hadn't meant to ask the question but was glad that she did when he seemed to collapse in on himself and reach for her.

'No,' he said, hugging her close. 'There's nothing going on between us.'

'The photograph...?'

'Opportunistic, no more. Fiona is getting married tomorrow. That's why I'm here.'

'I thought...'

'I know what you thought.' He held her at arm's length. 'I should've told you I was attending her wedding. Not many people know. I didn't want to ruin her big day by advertising the fact that her ex-lover, the Prince of Wales, was a guest.'

'They let me think the worst of you.'

'Horace would've told you if you'd confided in him. I would've told you if you'd tried to ring me back.'

She huffed in a breath. 'Is it always going to be like this – me being kept in the dark, drawing conclusions, acting like an idiot?'

'I can't insist that you trust me – not when I don't trust myself.'

'You can ask me.'

His eyes widened. *Could he do that*? He shook his head. 'It wouldn't be fair, Felicity. I can't make you any promises.'

She stiffened. 'That's a bit selfish.'

'I know.' He gave a rueful smile. 'I want my cake, *and* I want to eat it.'

'As I said... selfish.'

'At this moment, I don't want anyone but you. Is that enough?'

She honestly didn't know.

'Let me have a shower, and I'll sleep on it.'

'There's a room all ready for you. I'll get someone to show you up.'

She nodded, suddenly very exhausted. 'Can we talk in the morning?'

'Yes. I'll come and find you for breakfast.'

'Is the queen very angry?'

'Livid.' He gestured a footman forward. 'Fetch my fiancé's luggage from the car,' he said, then, to her – 'I don't suppose you packed something that would be suitable for a wedding?'

She shook her head. 'Just jeans and a couple of blouses.' Realisation dawned. 'You want to take me to Fiona's wedding?'

'Now, that you're here...'

'No... oh, most definitely, *no*.' She stepped back in horror. 'I couldn't do that.'

'I think you might have to.'

'But...'

'I can send someone to find you a decent outfit off the rack at one of the department stores. They can bring a selection to choose from.'

'Are you mad? I can't turn up uninvited.'

'You're going to be the next queen, Felicity. Get used to being accepted wherever you land. Fiona will be pleased to have you.'

'I'm sorry... I can't.' the very thought of it horrified her.

His voice took on a stern note. 'It'll look odd, if you come all the way here, and then don't attend. What will the press make of that?'

'Is that all you care about... what the press and the public think?'

'It's why we're getting married, isn't it?' he snapped back at her.

He was right. It was foolish of her to think otherwise.

'I'm sorry,' he said. 'I didn't mean to snap.' He pulled her close, once more. 'Please do this for me. Afterwards, we can talk properly... make some ground rules.'

She was too tired to argue. She nodded against his chest.

Upstairs, in a room that took her breath away, she sat on the edge of the bed and tried to digest the events of the day. Everything that had happened was all down to the fact that she couldn't trust him. She'd seen the photograph, and immediately believed the worst of him. She couldn't blame herself for that. It had been perfectly feasible to believe that he was simply responding to her own revelations to the press.

She knew that there would be more photographs, more stories, more conclusions jumped-to. Sometimes, the stories would be true, but all of them would ultimately hurt her.

Once more, she had to ask herself the question – could she live with it?

She'd thought that she could. Today had shown her that, perhaps, she couldn't.

Chapter Twenty-Nine

The most unusual and shocking moment of attending Fiona's wedding came at the reception. They'd dined well, and the bride and groom waltzed the first dance. Everyone was having a good time, and no one had paid particular attention to Felicity or Louis. It had been a strangely enjoyable experience for her, and she was glad she'd agreed to attend.

When Fiona approached her, and pulled her to the side, she'd been taken aback. The bride hadn't uttered a single word to her - despite having welcomed Louis with a kiss on the cheek after the ceremony and as the guests had filed into the dining hall - and she'd been quite relieved to have been kindly ignored.

As she was drawn away by the woman he'd once been intimate with, Louis could only look on with surprise. He'd wanted to follow, but Fiona had shaken her head and waved him off.

He dreaded what she might say. He'd succeeded in calming Felicity down and managed to reassure her that nothing untoward would happen at the wedding, and he was now having to stand by and watch as Fiona confided goodness knew what in her.

He imagined all sorts of horrors. He'd dated Fiona for three or four months a couple of years previously. They'd had a volatile relationship but had become the best of friends once the love affair had fizzled out. He could imagine the effect that some of the stories of his exploits – stories that had never hit the headlines – would have on Felicity. She was feeling pretty fragile, and it wouldn't take much to push her over the edge and have her walking away from him and their wedding.

He looked after them balefully. *Whatever will be, will be.*

'Sit here,' Fiona said, patting the back of a chair. 'It's a bit quieter, and no one will disturb us.'

She had a melodic voice, and there was a sweetness to it that Felicity found reassuring. She didn't think that she was about to be verbally attacked or maligned in any way.

Fiona pushed at her dress and struggled to sit down. She actually laughed as the skirt puffed up and almost swallowed her whole.

'Dreadful thing,' she said, punching and attempting to flatten it. 'I hope your dress isn't as much of a monster?'

Felicity shook her head. 'No train, and no frills. It's pretty plain.'

'My mother insisted on a princess look for my dress. She told me, if I couldn't be a princess in real life, I could be one on my wedding day.'

'You look very beautiful, Fiona.'

'Thank you. It's always nice to get a compliment.'

'It was a really special day. Thank you for having me.'

'Did you know that I invited you?' She looked at her evenly. 'I let Louis know last week that he was welcome to bring you.'

She shook her head. 'He didn't tell me.'

'That doesn't surprise me.'

'Why not?'

She shrugged. 'It's just not something he'd do... bring you to his lover's wedding.'

'You're his lover?'

She realised what she'd said and looked horrified. 'No... goodness, no. We haven't been lovers for years.'

'That's what he told me.'

'Do you believe him?'

'Of course. He has no need to lie to me.'

'Why, because you would be accepting of it... if it had been true?'

Felicity thinned her lips. The conversation was becoming much too personal.

'I'm sorry that I got snapped with him. I know how it must've made you feel.'

Felicity wasn't prepared to get into that. Her feelings weren't open for discussion.

'What is it you want, Fiona? Why this private little tete-a-tete?'

'I want to get to know you. Louis and I are very close. My marriage won't come between our friendship, and I was hoping that his, to you, wouldn't either.'

'I won't dictate who Louis can be friends with.'

'Are you open to being my friend, too, Felicity? I mean... I'd like to be your friend.'

She shrugged. 'I don't know you, and a brief conversation isn't going to change that.'

'No, you're right... of course, you are. I just wanted to sound you out.'

She didn't understand Fiona's motivation. It was her wedding day. She shouldn't be pre-occupied with making new friends. That could wait. Why the urgency?

'You're frowning at me,' Fiona said. 'I'm coming across as all weird.'

'A little, I suppose.'

'Sorry. I'm rather impulsive. Louis is probably having kittens wondering what we're talking about.' She glanced over at him and gave a cheeky wave. 'Look at him, he's on hot-bricks.'

Felicity kept her eyes straight ahead. She had no need to witness Louis' anxiety.

'What might he be wondering?'

'Oh, I don't know. I've kept a few of his secrets over the years.'

'I'm not interested in his secrets.'

'No, quite right. They're all in the past.'

'And that's where they'll remain.'

A small silence dropped between them. Felicity made to stand, but Fiona placed a hand on her knee. 'Don't go just yet.'

'I'm not sure there's anything more to say, Fiona. We can be friends... we'll have to see. I'm not adverse to the idea.'

'That's a relief. I know that Louis will follow your lead. If we're not friends, I think I'd end up losing him completely.'

Felicity didn't necessarily believe that to be a bad idea. She had a feeling that Fiona was a little bit in love with him.

It was as if she'd read her mind. 'I love my husband very much,' she said. 'Louis was never the man for me. I couldn't tame him.'

Felicity felt that strike home. She wasn't going to be able to tame him, either.

'He's different around you. I've kept an eye on the two of you from a distance. He really likes you. He hasn't really liked any of his other girlfriends. He likes me *now*... but not so much when we were dating.'

'That's good to know.' She hoped the sarcasm wasn't lost on her.

'Oh, don't get me wrong... I'm sure he *more than* likes you. After all, he's marrying you, and you were childhood sweethearts, of a sort.'

She simply sat and stared at her. She was unsure where the conversation was going.

'I want to give you some advice,' she said. 'And don't look at me like that. I mean well.'

'Everyone wants to give me advice,' Felicity returned. 'it's never welcome.'

'Okay... you can ignore it, but please let me give it.'

'It's your day... you can say what you want.'

She thought a moment. 'Two things, really – and please don't take offence.'

'I won't.'

'Right.' She steeled herself. 'First – don't be too clingy. He hates clingy women.'

'And second?'

'Let him be himself. Don't turn him into something he's not.'

'Is that it?'

She bit her lip and nodded.

Felicity stood and walked away on very unsteady legs.

Chapter Thirty

When she returned to his side, he was conscious of the paleness of her cheeks. He was truly fearful of what she'd just been told. Fiona knew things about him that Felicity might not understand. They weren't terrible things, simply embarrassing and best left unsaid. He didn't want to look bad in her eyes. He already did – for a number of reasons, not least his poor judgement when he'd dumped her so cruelly all those years before – and he didn't want to further reduce her opinion of him.

He wondered why it mattered. She knew what she was taking on, and a few misdemeanours as a young adult shouldn't make a blind bit of difference. But it *did* matter, and it *would* make a difference.

He didn't ask her, and she didn't offer. It seemed that what had been said between them would remain between them. He was pleased that she didn't act cool towards him. In fact, she was quite warm and attentive, and he soon put his worries behind him and relaxed.

Louis knew most of the wedding guests, and Felicity was a nodding acquaintance of one or two of them. Their society was a small one, and it wasn't surprising that she recognised a schoolfriend, or someone who was a friend of a friend.

She accepted offers to dance. One man – known to Louis, but not to her – danced with her on no less than three occasions. The third time she accepted, she thought she saw a thunderous expression on Louis' face, but she shrugged it off as meaning nothing.

Louis only danced with her. He had no interest in the bridesmaids, or any of the female guests. As the evening turned into night, he found his eyes resting on Felicity more and more, and for longer and longer periods.

She now had a bit of colour about her, and he was glad to see her enjoying herself. Sometimes, he minded her giving herself to others. It was only a dance, or a snatched conversation, but he felt the stirrings of jealousy whenever she failed to glance across at him or look as if she minded being away from his side.

He'd been jealous only once before, and that had nothing to do with a woman. His father had given his sister his favourite polo pony. Louis loved that pony and had often ridden him in matches. If anyone should've been gifted that pony, it should've been him. He still wasn't sure what his father's motivation was for deliberately upsetting him. He knew that his sister wasn't interested. She couldn't have cared less about the pony, whereas Louis had cherished it.

He never rode the pony again, and he never really forgave his father that one churlish act.

A tight band wound around his chest as he watched her dance with Lawrence Collinsworth for the third time. As far as he was concerned, it was two too many times to witness her in that man's arms. He almost rose and strode over to cut in. Lawrence would object, and there would be a scene, so he stayed put and simmered.

When he saw them whispering as they stepped off the dancefloor, that simmer rose almost to a full boil. *What was all that about*? He shuddered to think.

She sat down at his side, fanning a hand in front of her face. Lawrence gave a courtly bow, winked at her, and turned to leave. Louis thought that he might punch him in the face if he came calling again.

'You okay?' she asked him. 'Only you look a bit put out.'

'I'm fine,' he snapped. He rounded on her. 'What were you two whispering about?'

'Whispering? Who?'

'You and Lawrence.'

'Were we whispering?'

He couldn't decide if she was genuinely confused, or if she was toying with him.

'Forget it,' he said, turning away.

She put a hand on his arm, and he turned to face her once more.

'It was nothing,' she said. 'Just something silly.'

'If you say so.'

She smiled at his mulish look. If she hadn't known any better, she would think that he was jealous.

'Oh, my goodness,' she almost squealed. 'It's *Lady in Red*... it's our song. Let's dance.' She pulled him to his feet.

Our song? Yes, he thought – *it is our song*.

Lady in Red was followed immediately by James Blunt's *You're Beautiful*, and he held her close, inhaled her scent, and savoured every moment of the two songs in her arms.

When they were sitting in the back of the car, heading back to Holyrood House, he realised – for the first time – that he more than liked her. It scared him. He didn't know how to deal with it so, when they said goodnight, he was brusque, and she thought he was still upset with her over the whispering episode.

Neither of them slept well that night. Both were bleary-eyed and irritable in the morning.

Apart from a curt *good morning*, breakfast was conducted in silence. Louis buried his face in his smart phone, and Felicity sat in a daze staring at her fried egg and button mushrooms, not understanding what was going on between them.

They'd had a wonderful day at the wedding. Fiona had nearly spoiled it for her, but she'd ended up having a fun time. Louis was attentive and gave her free rein to enjoy herself. She'd seen him relaxed amongst his friends, and she'd felt like a queen at his side, particularly because he didn't share his attention with any other women.

She'd obviously upset him. She'd gone to bed thinking that he'd been jealous of the attention Lawrence had paid her, but ultimately disbelieved that because that simply wasn't Louis' style. He wouldn't know what jealousy was if it punched him in the guts, and – even if he was familiar with it – why should he be jealous of anyone paying attention to her?

Rich people were often possessive of their possessions. Was that it? Did he think he owned her?

She pushed her plate to the side and cleared her throat.

He looked up from his phone and raised an eyebrow.

'You said we could talk... lay down some ground rules,' she said. 'Can we do it now?'

'Later. I'm a bit busy.' He dropped his eyes back to the screen.

'It's now, or never, Louis. We're heading back to London in an hour. It will be too late, then.'

'Too late for what?'

'To talk. To reach an understanding.'

'You want to discuss an open marriage?'

'What? No! Don't be ridiculous.'

'I just thought – with Lawrence showing an interest, and you lapping it up...' He left the rest unsaid.

She laughed, and it was the worst thing she could have done. His reaction was way over the top. He stood, kicked his chair back, and stormed from the room.

Stunned, she looked after him open-mouthed. This was a new Louis. *Where had he come from, and what the blazes was wrong with him*?

She didn't get to find out. He left before her, leaving her to travel back with Charles and Ronald.

She fumed the whole way back to London, slammed into the house, and locked herself in her bedroom. He'd given her no reason for leaving without her, made no apology, and ignored every attempt she'd made to contact him.

She was not to know that he too, was locked in his bedroom, suffering much as she was, and just as confused.

Both sets of parents spent an anxious few days wondering if the wedding was going to go ahead.

Chapter Thirty-One

A sort of uncomfortable truce existed between them during the final week before the wedding. They'd spoken only twice since arriving back from Edinburgh. The first time, it was to agree that they would go through with the marriage, and – as Louis put it – *learn how to be man and wife on the job*.

The second time was to confirm the rehearsal. It was planned for that evening, and Felicity wasn't looking forward to it. She dreaded seeing him. She thought that they were skating on very thin ice, and that it wouldn't take much for everything to crash and burn. She wanted to marry him more than ever. Her love for him hadn't been marred by his strange behaviour. She felt that she could forgive him almost anything, but she wasn't so sure that he wanted it to go ahead as much as she did. Things had gone completely topsy-turvy. They'd began the whole affair with a reluctant bride, and now they had a reluctant bridegroom. Instead of her not trusting him, he didn't trust her.

Following him to Scotland had been a mistake. It was obvious that he'd seen a side to her that he didn't like. All that nonsense about an open marriage, and Lawrence being thrown into the equation was ludicrous, and was merely a symptom of something else that was eating at him.

If only they had the opportunity for some alone-time. Talking things through and finding enough trust to give them a fighting chance, was all she wanted, but Louis was always too busy, or otherwise unavailable.

The media had decided to be kind to her. Robert Baker hadn't come out of the woodwork to deny her statement, and everyone was, at last, looking forward with excitement to the big day.

Louis didn't turn up for the rehearsal. A last-minute emergency kept him away. His non-appearance hurt her far more than words could describe.

She went through the motions without him and went back home with the black blanket of depression slowly enfolding her.

'Louis is downstairs,' her mother said. 'He says it's urgent.'

This was it, she thought. *He's calling it off.*

She trudged downstairs and almost didn't go into the drawing room. She had to give him credit for turning up to tell her straight to her face. He needn't have done that. He could've quite easily got Horace, or one of the flunkeys to tell her.

She stepped into the room and closed the door. She was shocked by his haggard expression. It obviously pained him to have to deliver the news himself.

'Sit down, Felicity,' he said. 'This is going to come as a bit of a shock.'

'I'll stand,' she said, guardedly.

'Well, I'm going to sit. I'm still a little dazed.'

Dazed? She looked at him as he threw himself onto the sofa. He certainly looked dazed. That didn't quite fit with what she'd expected.

'What's going on, Louis? You didn't turn up for the rehearsal, and you turn up here... *dazed*?'

'I'm sorry about the rehearsal. It couldn't be helped.'

'Is the queen all right?'

'Not really. She's had a bit of a shock.'

'Something to do with me... with us?'

'Indirectly.'

'For goodness' sake, Louis... spit it out.' She joined him on the sofa. 'Get it over with. Did you tell your mother that you won't marry me? Is that what shocked her?'

'No.' He looked alarmed. 'Is that why you think I'm here – to call it off?'

'Why else?'

'Because of Horace?'

'What?' She shifted back. 'Horace?'

He focussed his gaze on her. 'He's responsible for Robert Baker.'

She wobbled and dropped back against the cushion. He reached out a hand to steady her.

'He blackmailed him.'

'What?' *Get a grip, Felicity. Say something more than what.*

'He has a cousin who Baker managed probate for. Apparently, he somehow fiddled the books and charged an exorbitant amount for the work. I think he broke more than a few ethical laws. Horace found out and used the information to make Baker admit to having an affair with you.'

'Why?'

'Because he doesn't want me to be king. He's in cahoots with the Prime Minister and didn't want the marriage to go ahead. He didn't consider, for a moment, that I'd believe your side of the story.'

'But all that happened before there even was a wedding planned.'

'He hoped to scupper it before I persuaded you to accept my proposal.'

'How... how did you find out?'

'Baker came clean. That's why I didn't make the rehearsal. He managed to get a hold of me and explained the whole thing. I think his wife made him come forward. He's more terrified of her than being struck-off, or disbarred... whatever you call it.' He smiled for the first time. 'You should've seen Horace's face when I confronted him. He ran to mother – hoping she'd back him – but she gave him short-shrift.'

'I'm glad you know... that it wasn't true.'

'I always knew, Felicity.'

'Always?'

'Well, I might've wobbled at first, but I know you too well to believe that of you.'

'Thank you.'

'What are you thanking *me* for?'

'Believing in me.'

He looked away.

'What's wrong, Louis? Something is broken between us. It's obvious.'

'Just pre-wedding jitters.'

'Look at me when you say that.'

He turned to face her. 'Honestly... I'm just a bit spooked. I've never been married before.'

'Are you sure?'

He put an arm around her and dragged her over beside him. 'I'm sure.'

She sighed with relief. 'You had me worried.'

'I've been a bit of a jerk. I don't mind admitting it.'

'If I've got this wrong... forgive me, but were you jealous?'

He wanted to deny it. He was embarrassed. He said, 'I'm always going to be honest with you. No matter what – you'll always get the truth, okay?'

She chewed on her lip and nodded.

'I was eaten up with jealousy.' He stared deep into her eyes. 'I hated another man's arms being around you, and I hated that you found Lawrence amusing. I envied the ease in which you whispered and smiled. I was so jealous I couldn't think straight.'

'How lovely,' she said, moving in to kiss him. 'That's the nicest thing you've ever said to me.'

Epilogue

The wedding ceremony didn't go as planned. Louis introduced something to the proceedings that had never been done before. He'd told the archbishop of his intentions, and he was the only one in the know.

The headlines called it unprecedented. It ran on a loop over and over again on the world's televisions for days afterwards.

When there was a hush. When the right moment was presented to him, Louis spoke his vows.

They weren't rehearsed. They weren't part of the traditional royal wedding ceremony. They caused Felicity to cry.

He turned to her, took both of her hands in his, and gazed at her lovingly.

'I love you,' he said, for everyone to hear. 'I vow to always love you. I will be faithful, and true, and never cause you a moment's pain. I will strive to be worthy of you, and I will spend every day of my life making you happy.'

He meant every single word, and – as corny as it may sound - they lived happily ever after.

I hope you enjoyed Louis and Felicity's story. Please consider rating or reviewing it. Your opinion will matter to others who might like to read the book, and I would appreciate it.

If you want to read more English Prince romances, the author has two more published:

The English Prince and the American

And

An English Prince Comes to Dinner

Thank you for reading The English Prince and the Reluctant Bride.
If you enjoyed the book, please consider leaving a rating or a review.
Other books in the English Prince series:
The English Prince and the American
An English Prince Comes to Dinner
The English Prince and the Bad Girl
An English Prince for Sale